Mr. M's Notebook
A Teacher's Life

A Trilogy
By John Splaine

Published by Piscataqua Press
An imprint of RiverRun Bookstore
142 Fleet Street | Portsmouth NH | 03801
www.riverrunbookstore.com
www.piscataquapress.com

ISBN: 978-1-944393-25-0
Printed in the United States of America

For Pam:
Daughter, Granddaughter, Sister, Wife, Mother,
Grandmother, Educator, Friend, and Teacher.

And,

Mr. M's Notebook: A Teacher's Life is a gift to my
teachers, colleagues, and students.

And,

To my parents, who taught me what teacher
means.

Thanks to my reviewers. I thank you. J. S.

Mark Blenchard taught in Bailey T. S. Memorial High School for almost fifty years. This is his story. Book one takes us from 1970 to the mid 1980's. Book two will carry us through the rest of the 1980's and the decade of the 1990's. Book three starts in 2000 and brings us to the present.

Table of Contents

Book One:

Bailey High

Chapter 1:
Derek

"*D*erek, damn it! Why did you do it? You have to know better than that. You are a good teacher, the students love you and you do a great job in the classroom. I just don't get it. What exactly did you do and why in hell did you do it?"

Derek was, indeed, a good teacher. I did not want to lose him.

I have taught history and social studies at Bailey T. S. Memorial High School in Gorham, Massachusetts, since 1970. I started teaching in the fall after I graduated from college.

In 1973, three years after I joined the school's faculty, the chair of the department I was in retired. I became the chair more by default than because I had earned it. It was early in my career but I felt ready enough. Besides, I had a growing family. I needed the extra money that came with being the chair, so I was glad nobody else wanted the job. I wasn't sure what I was getting into. However, I considered the boost in income and there was some prestige in being the history and social studies department chair. Most of Bailey High's faculty concurred with me that the department was a good one with effective teachers. I took the task on. I had little idea of what the job required, but I was ready and willing.

1

I got married in the summer of 1970. By the fall of 1973, my son Joel was 3 years old and my daughter Suzie was approaching her first birthday. The children liked to eat and the additional cash as chair would help feed them. With two children, I found that I needed every dollar. I walked into the assignment without a smidgen of an idea of what I was getting into.

When Derek Randallston found himself in trouble in April of 1975, I had to deal with it because I was the chair. I knew the superintendent of schools would be calling. He did not welcome controversy in his school system. And, Derek's situation could easily become public. Mitchell Appletone, the superintendent, did not like anyone criticizing his school system, anyone at all, for any reason.

"What did you do Derek?" I asked again.

Derek stuttered a response, "I was in my car with Lydia and a police officer approached my car."

"Lydia Smith, who is in your senior history class?"

"Yes. She is 18, I checked."

"What does it matter what her age is and what do you mean you checked? Are you asking for trouble? You have to know that having a student in a parked car is not a good idea regardless of the age." I said, not believing what I was hearing.

"What happened in the car?" I asked afraid of what I might hear.

"What do you mean what happened?" Derek replied.

"Come on Derek, you are playing with me. You know what I mean."

"Well, nothing happened. We were in the car alone talking."

"Derek, I have got to know the whole story. Then what happened?"

"Well, then a male officer came over to the car."

"A policeman? One? Derek, it is the end of spring break and

a parked car in a dark area probably attracted him. So, he came over?"

"Yes, Mark, it was just one, just one policeman came over."

"What did the cop see and what did he say?"

"He just saw us sitting there. He asked us what we were doing there. Nothing was really happening."

"Nothing!" I spit out as my skepticism oozed out. I was getting more anxious by the moment. "Come on, Derek, I need to know. And what was the talk about?" I asked, knowing that I would need to find out what happened to see if Derek's job could be salvaged.

"Nothing special. We were just talking about things. But, she did say something that made me think of things. I didn't answer though, and I never touched her."

"So, you were just talking about 'things' as you put it. What happened next?"

"Nothing. We were just talking. The policeman said he was going to talk to the superintendent of schools about me being alone in a car with a student."

"Oh, damn, I can't believe you did this Derek. You have exceeded being naïve. Don't you know better than to be sitting in a parked car in a darkened area in the middle of April at the end of spring break with a high school student? You are a smart guy in the classroom. How can you be so clueless outside of it?"

"But Mark, nothing happened. We were just talking."

"Sure, right—just talking. And, we expect the superintendent to believe that!"

"Well, Mark, it is the truth, nothing happened."

"I want to believe you, Derek. In fact, I have to. I may be a fool but I want to save your job as a teacher. You have helped a lot of students, and your colleagues value what you do in the classroom."

"Thanks Mark, that means a lot to me. I want to keep my

job. I love teaching."

"But Derek, it may not matter what you and I think or want to have happen. You were in that car with Lydia Smith and shouldn't have been."

Chapter 2:
Mitchell

*O*n Friday afternoon at the end of spring break, I received a message that I should call the superintendent of school's office. Superintendent Mitchell Appletone worked twenty-four-seven so it was not unusual that he or someone in his office would call during the break. Because it was coming to the end of the term, I was busy grading papers and compiling grades. I figured responding to the inquiry could wait. I assumed the superintendent's call was regarding a parent asking about an assignment or asking a question about a grade.

Derek called me on Saturday morning. He asked to meet with me privately at my house. After meeting with Derek about the policeman coming upon his parked car with Lydia Smith and Derek in it, I had a better idea of what the superintendent's call was most likely about. The policeman must have contacted the superintendent of schools and told him that he saw Derek Randallston, a teacher in Bailey High, in a parked car at night with a student. If that was what the call was all about, I decided to go to the superintendent's office to meet in person on Monday morning rather than talk over the phone.

I knew the superintendent would be working customarily early so I went to meet with him to see what his call was about. He did not take spring breaks, or many breaks for that matter.

5

He toiled through holidays and the spring and summer breaks, so I thought he would be in his office early on the Monday after spring break as school started again. Mitchell was always in his office, so I went to see him shortly after 6 a.m.

As I walked toward his office, I remembered that on Mondays he had a service club breakfast meeting, so I didn't expect to find him there quite this early. However, on this particular Monday, the light in his office was burning bright. I had a hunch as to why.

Mitchell and I were on a first name basis. We were cordial with each other, but we were not drinking buddies. Occasionally, we did have coffee together when we came across each other in the local bakery.

Mitchell had been the district superintendent for over two decades. He had seen a lot happen in the district's schools. He liked to control what was happening on his watch.

Mitchell's appearance signaled much about him. Mitchell carefully arranged his bowties. He never wore anything else. His attention to neatness bordered on zealotry. He spent an inordinate amount of time fussing, even obsessing, over his sparse hair. On more than one occasion, I had seen Mitchell carefully coif his remaining strands over his multiple bald spots. He bristled when people referred to him as "balding." School system employees soon learned to refrain from ever using the word bald in his presence. When Mitchell was not in earshot, we would use the term balderdash to convey the message that he was attempting a new cover up.

Mitchell's puffed ego and hubris led him to attend fastidiously to his meticulous dress. His shirts, invariably starched, had the look of being new. The rigid crease in his pants matched his demeanor. Yet, Mitchell's body fit more than snugly into his clothes. He spent a lot of time in the gym. He was not a runner—he lifted weights instead—often. However, his addiction to donuts expanded his belt size yearly.

Mitchell's love for donuts added a bulge to what must have been an endlessly growing forty-plus-inch waist. His donut-inflated belly made his belts looked like they were two inches longer than his stomach. Hanging loosely from his pants' loops, this gave the appearance that Mitchell's gut had room to grow. His vanity wore thin even if his midriff did not.

We all seem to fill our lives with contradictions. Mitchell was no exception. He developed his multiple personalities into high art. He worked out frantically and regularly, yet he added fat to the stomach he tried so hard to contain. Mitchell complained about others who had wide girths while his widened. Indeed, Mitchell's many oxymoronic views and habits spawned lines in his observers' foreheads. It wasn't Mitchell's weight that bothered me because I had my own expanded pant size—it was his hypocrisy about almost everything. Mitchell had perfected pecking away at everyone else's peccadillos but never his.

Mitchell and his wife, Winnie, did not have any children that we knew of. No one on the faculty had ever met Winnie. We just assumed she existed. Mitchell once told me in one of his more candid moments, "Mark, you will never be a superintendent of schools. You have children. That indicates that you are not serious about running a school system. I work all the time at my job. You would have to too. But with kids, you just wouldn't have the time." I didn't bother to tell him that I did not ever want to be a superintendent because it might make me more like him.

When he believed he would not be found out, Mitchell expressed an affinity for attractive women. He was an inveterate ogler. He had an eye for what he called "the ladies." Although, his "ladies" had to fit his definition of attractive—"thin and very thin." Indeed, Mitchell's ideal woman would most likely have to live life without consuming as many donuts as he did.

As Mitchell looked and looked, his peering eyes expressed feigned desire. Mitchell, for all his desirous gawking, conveyed an asexual persona. He personified the "dirty old man." He looked, he peered, and he ogled— but did not seem to want to do more—just look—maybe a surreptitious touch now and then, but no more. He was a strange man. No one seemed to know him. I knew I did not.

Mitchell was as firm with people as his face was taut. If you did what he wanted you to do, then he was considered to be fair. If you weren't doing what he wanted you to do, then his infamous temper flared into a blistering tirade. Even though I had never seen or personally experienced his emotional blusters, I heard stories of his "dressing down" employees. I had only experienced his quiet rage, which was trauma enough.

A stubborn streak followed his tantrums. Once you were on Mitchell's bad side then you stayed there. Clearly, if this visit was to be about Derek, then Derek had gone way outside Mitchell's "what I want you to do red line."

As I entered the superintendent's outer office, I walked slowly past Judy Bain, the receptionist. She waved me past her desk with a look indicating that it was not just okay but necessary for me to go in to Mitchell Appletone's office immediately. Ms. Bain was an early-riser. She echoed Mitchell's comportment. He wanted his employees to be his alter ego—Judy Bain engulfed the challenge.

I knocked lightly on Mitchell's office door and began turning the door handle. Mitchell knew that it must be me. He said in his angry as hell, all-business, muffled roar of a voice, "Come in Mark." It was clear that I better go in quickly. I did. I feared this might be my first encounter with the infamous temper.

Before we even exchanged greetings, Mitchell's booming voice bellowed: "He has got to go." Mitchell didn't smile much and he was not smiling now. "Mark, I am assuming I do not have to tell you what I am talking about. It is that Randallston guy. Of course, you know who the heck I mean."

"Yes, I do."

I was not surprised with the no-nonsense but was stunned by the resounding finality of the directive. I was still just standing there as Mitchell continued, "I presume I do not have to tell you why."

"Well, there was no physical contact as far as I know."

"Mark. Darn it." Mitchell again came as close to profanity as he ever did, indicating how angry he was. "He has to go. Ask him to resign. No, tell him to resign. If Randallston resigns, I will not make it public. If anyone asks me for a recommendation I will tell them that I cannot give one and leave it at that. If it becomes public, well..."

"Alright, Mitchell, I will tell him." I knew that when Mitchell made up his mind that there was no changing it. His mind was made up now. Derek had to go, and go soon.

Mitchell possessed the fiduciary power. He should be the one to tell Derek that he was fired. I wanted to tell the superintendent that it was his job to tell Derek that he would no longer teach at Bailey High. However, Mitchell would not do it himself, and candid feedback to this superintendent was taboo and met with retaliation. He used surrogates to handle unpleasant duties. I was the designated surrogate in this case.

Mitchell excelled in brow beating others to execute his directives. However, if I made a mistake Mitchell would blame the messenger and absolve himself of any blame. His mantra was "It is your fault and you better take care of it." My teacher-friends in other schools said Mitchell Appletone was an anomaly among school superintendents and that most of them

9

were good educators. I looked forward to working with a student-oriented superintendent someday.

I left Mitchell's office with a resigned nod to Ms. Bain. She barely looked up from her desk, but her askance glance made it clear that she grasped the fact her boss's business needed to be done and that I had better do it if I wanted to keep my job. I had a wife and two children, so I did need the job.

Mitchell controlled the school board. He had sown favors among the school board members—each and every one. They owed Mitchell. He knew it and the school board members knew it. Some of the more prominent and powerful members owed him big-time for favors done for family and friends. As a result of the benefits that had been bestowed, Mitchell had neutralized those board members who could otherwise have opposed him. So, any appeals to the school board would be met by stony silence and well-developed looks of practiced resignation.

In Mitchell Appletone's world, there was no room for error— no room at all. He was the boss in a world of bosses. I realized I had to get to Derek as soon as I could. I had to do what the boss said or I would be toast too. Any guts I had already excreted.

Chapter 3:
"Mr. D."

I returned to the school realizing that what must be done needed to be executed quickly and by me. Derek was a star teacher. He littered his classroom with good open questions guiding his students to think critically and beyond the conventional. He sprinkled through his students the Who, What, Where, When, How, and mostly the Why of issues. Students invariably named Mr. D. as their favorite teacher who taught them the most and prepared them on how to adjust to what the future held.

In the late 1960's, teachers and students in Bailey T. S. Memorial High School decided that calling teachers Mr., Miss., and Mrs., and the teacher's last name was too formal and that first names alone were too informal, so the students at the school started to affectionately (mostly) call teachers by Mr. and Ms. and then the first initial of their first name. Thus, Derek was Mr. D., and when I became a teacher in Bailey High, the students declared I was to be "thenceforth—Mr. M."

Even though college students returning to Bailey for a visit frequently proclaimed Derek as the teacher who helped them to be prepared for college-level work and life in general, and regardless of the good work he had accomplished teaching in Bailey, Derek still had to go. A policeman had discovered him in a car with a student, and a determined Mitchell Appletone wanted to get him out of Bailey High—pronto. And, get him out he would, one way or another—with or without my assistance.

Bailey T. S. Memorial High School sits in the middle of Gorham, Massachusetts. As with some other communities in Massachusetts, Gorham's historic roots reach deep. The town takes its history seriously. When told by the locals, Gorham's history captivates and captures natives and visitors alike. In the town, history glows romantically—deserved or not. Over the years, embellishments infiltrated the story's telling.

A river runs adjacent to the town. Streams and over-flow slice through and separate Gorham's neighborhoods. The town's residents had throughout its history lived off the water which fed the mills' machinery and other industry. A "River Walk" now leads tourists to fashionable restaurants and shops.

The wealthier people in town live on the higher ground—the poorer closer to the flood plain. The elementary schools are segregated by housing patterns. Children living in the low income part of town go to school with children from a similar economic background. The progeny of the higher income parents attend school with children from comparable demographics. Wealthy families, with the means and desire to do so, send their children to private schools in adjacent communities.

Money can be made in the city by the river. In the 1950's, Gorham adopted "River City" as its pseudonym. Millennials and aging "wannabe" hippies with dollars overflowing their pockets mix in the bars and trendy eating places during the day as partying slides effortlessly into the evening. Finding someone to be with for a night has become increasingly easy to do as the patrons at the "watering holes" drink and drink some more. The locals, for the most part, like having the visitors around, enjoying the tips left behind. Gorham's restaurant employees and the townspeople who own them exclaim disingenuous "Good byes," and "Thanks for coming" when nomads leave to go back to where they belong.

Gorham houses blue collar as well as white collar workers who commute to Boston, the technological Route 28 corridor, and the greater Boston environs. In elections, the town's people vote mostly for conservative candidates. The town's residents have refined orthodoxy and conformity. They choose their social strictures carefully. They disgorge anything approaching libertine behavior.

The town's politicians boast that Gorham is not like some of the more liberal communities in the state where "leftist" policies rule. In Gorham, blue and white collars remain the standard. Hence, the sixties' counter- culture types could come into town to spend their money, but Gorham's residents prefer that the tie-dyed sleep elsewhere.

So, it was clear to me that if the Superintendent of Schools in this community wanted Derek to go fast— like right now— then it was going to be a done deal. There would be no debate in this town when it came to crossing the lines of social conformity.

Mitchell knew that the rumor mill worked fast in Gorham. Mitchell did not mind rumors as long as he was the one generating them. I did not have to be keenly politically aware to realize that Derek was in trouble. I grasped the urgency of the mess Derek had created in this community at this time. There was no hiding from the "Scarlet Letter," especially in this conservative Massachusetts town.

Mitchell was in charge and could smell the odor of a potential imbroglio much less a scandal. Over time, he had measured the sentiment in Gorham. Mitchell seethed when he sensed that political opprobrium might be directed toward him. He was all too willing to ride along with the political winds in whichever direction they were blowing or about to. If the school board ever got the drift of Derek's indiscretion, then there would be hell to pay. Mitchell did not like paying for anything, much less for the hell that the news of Derek's alleged immoral behavior could engender.

So, things had to occur quickly and quietly. I raced to school and then upstairs to find Derek before the first period. He was about to be in Mitchell's words— "done and gone." The "boss" did not want Derek to even teach his first period class, much less be around when the post-spring break school day started. Mitchell demanded Derek be run out of town by sun down. Gorham's social structure made it a "Sundown town" for those who violated its written and unwritten rules. Derek had leaned against its verboten wall. Woe to those who try to crack it, or even mistakenly nudge the hamlet's taboos.

I planned to take over his first period class. Derek did not have a second period class. We would have to find a substitute for the third period. The assistant principal had a list of possible substitutes who could make it in to school on the spur of the moment, so with a little time we could cover the rest of Derek's class schedule. After Derek was gone, we would try to hire a long term substitute or someone as a permanent replacement.

I found Derek in his carrel preparing for class as was his practice. He was invariably well prepared when he walked into his classes. I motioned to him that we needed to talk privately. I did not have a first period class so we went to my usual classroom where we would have some privacy. I got right to the point, "Derek, the superintendent is adamant, he wants you out and he wants you out now. He wants your resignation or he will go public which would make it difficult, if not impossible, for you to get a teaching job or maybe any good job elsewhere. You have to leave—soon! Actually, you should leave now."

Derek's body sank, freezing his heart. Through his choked throat, a vibrating, emotion-filled voice spit words barely audible, "But, I love teaching. I do not want to leave my students. I didn't do anything. I didn't touch a student. I didn't do anything wrong."

"I understand what you are saying. I know you love teaching, are good at it, and don't want to leave." After pausing to compose myself, I continued, "Over the time I have known you, you have shown how much you care about teaching and value your students. But..."

After we talked for a few minutes, Derek recognized that he probably would have to leave the school, and if nothing came out publicly that he would have a chance to teach at another school maybe in another state. Kids talk, but he could claim later that there was nothing on his record and that if anyone said anything he could say that it was just unsubstantiated rumor. And, if he left now, there would be no formal record. I told him that Mitchell said he would not say anything if Derek left now without making any fuss. I said to Derek, "Any resistance would just make matters worse—much worse."

Derek had tucked some money away so he could support himself for a while. His father succeeded as an insurance agent. His mother had taught elementary school until the children came along. Derek's parents had invested wisely. Both Derek and his brother went to selective, private colleges. The Randallston family possessed resources. Derek could survive without a job, but he did not want just a job, he wanted this job.

Derek didn't want to leave teaching even briefly but he now realized that he would have to. He believed he did nothing wrong, but he should not have made the mistake of being in the car alone with Lydia at night. There was no way to turn that clock back.

This was all painful for both of us. Derek was at the high school when I came in 1970. The first thing I heard when I arrived at Bailey High was how good a teacher Derek was. I wanted to be a good teacher like him, so I spent time in his classroom observing how he taught. We talked for hours after school and on some weekends. I got to know him well.

Derek was single and I was newly married when we first met. He explained his background to me and how he got into teaching. When he was a high school student, he got the reputation (part complimentary and partly pejorative) of being a "nerd."

Derek was about five feet six inches tall with a protruding nose. He wore black rimmed classes in an apparent attempt to divert attention from his nose. He was self-conscious about his facial features although he looked fine to his colleagues and his students. None of the faculty or his students ever joked about Derek's looks or made comments, but Derek was overly concerned about what he looked like.

To the school's populace, Derek was just Mr. D. Yet, Derek Randallston's concern about his face affected him manifesting itself in insecurity, even in his teaching. He became solicitous of positive feedback even when he did not have to. He was good at what he did. He just didn't know it. Maybe he never would. His preoccupation with his physical appearance affected the rest of him.

Students found Derek's dry humor both entertaining and instructive. The students, who could sometimes be mean about such things, never mentioned "his looks." When students were heard talking about Mr. D., they invariably talked about a teacher they liked. They would comment about how much they learned in his class. Mr. D. was also well known for his joke of the day which kept the students loose and laughing even when the subjects discussed in class were serious. Derek always seemed to be on topic—intent about teaching and doing it well with a dash of humor.

Derek joined the high school faculty in 1967, three years before I did. In social studies, he had a lot to work with in the late 1960's and work it he did. In 1967 alone, thousands marched in San Francisco against the Vietnam War as Martin Luther King spoke out against the violence in a war-torn nation. At this juncture, the fighting in Vietnam had resulted in over 15,000 Americans dead as the war heated and expanded.

Also in 1967, President Lyndon B. Johnson nominated Thurgood Marshall to the Supreme Court of the United States. After Senate confirmation, Marshall became the first African American justice of the Supreme Court of the United States. Times were changing.

Nineteen sixty-eight also saw the North Vietnamese army launch an invasion into American backed South Vietnam—the so-called "Tet Offensive." It became clear that the situation in Vietnam was reaching the crisis stage in that fateful year. The media's growing echo-phone spread the national angst.

In the fateful year of 1968, a gunman assassinated Martin Luther King, Jr. in April. The murder traumatized Americans. Running for president, Robert F. Kennedy Jr. also died from an assassin's bullet in June. During the nation's turbulent presidential election in 1968, Republican Richard M. Nixon defeated Democrat Hubert H. Humphrey to become the president of the United States. Nixon's election would have profound implications for events in the beginning years of the 1970's.

Indeed, 1968 was the critical year as the 1960's morphed into the equally newsworthy 1970's. Yet, in 1969, Americans had something to cheer about as their compatriots landed the "Eagle" in the Sea of Tranquility on the moon and took "One giant leap for mankind." And, no less important and prescient of days yet to come, gays fought back at the Stonewall Inn in New York City.

By the end of the decade, American dead in far off Vietnam approached 40,000. So, in the late 1960's, Derek worked a plethora of issues into discussions in his social studies classes. Cognitive excitement threaded throughout his class debates and discussions. In class, Derek and his students thoughtfully tried to determine where the United States and the world were going, and what role each student might have in the future.

When I arrived at the school in the fall of 1970, I heard about Derek's skillful teaching concerning these sensitive and controversial issues. I studied Derek as a model teacher, tried to emulate what I learned from him, and maybe be nearly as good as he was in the classroom.

Yes, indeed, I wanted to be like Derek in the classroom. Nevertheless, he had crossed that invisible line separating teacher and student. I thought about calling someone, anyone, for advice on what to do. Derek's magic in the classroom is hard to find. We had no one to replace him and to duplicate what he did with students. We may be unable to find anyone nearly as good. Mitchell's timeline for Derek's departure was short. I lacked the time to call anyone for help in what I should do. Ultimately, it was my Mitchell-mandated task to tell Derek he had to go. I didn't want to, but I had to do it.

Chapter 4:
"Too Cool"

*D*erek and I talked frequently during the almost five years I knew him. We had so many personal and professional conversations that I considered him a friend as well as a teacher I respected.

When I started teaching in Bailey High, I had a lot to learn as a novice teacher. I learned much about teaching by being in and observing Derek's classroom. I had hoped to learn more as his colleague through the years.

Derek reported to me that when he was in secondary school, he obeyed the rules and did, "Exactly what I was instructed to do. I was already a committed and disciplined student in the private independent, co-educational school I attended. I was a good boy and did what I was told. I was a total conformist. I guess I still am. I did what others wanted and expected me to do. I seldom went up against the line of social acceptance, and never really challenged conventional behavior. I was, by and large, a 'nice' guy. Maybe too nice."

One of our conversations became particularly personal and revealing. Derek confided, "I did not date anyone in my four years of high school. Others went to the proms but I did not. I always found an excuse for not attending school dances or having other social interactions with females at the school. I worried about being rejected and that people would laugh at me."

Explaining further, Derek opened up telling more than I thought I needed to know. "I had a few sexual experiences during high school but they were with other guys, not with girls." This was not something readily admitted in the late 1960's and early 1970's. Homosexual contact or anything resembling it was still frowned upon socially and in some places illegal. If you did engage with a person of the same sex, then you kept it hush-hush. In the early 1970's, even a trace of homosexual talk, never mind behavior, breached community norms, and could get you in social and legal trouble. Friends suddenly ignored you—public officials watched more closely.

During the time I knew Derek, and when we were both growing up, any hint of homosexuality was anathema. His admission, therefore, surprised me. You could be "horny" when it came to girls because that was considered to be okay and the way guys were supposed to be. Exhibiting one's desire for sex with females, especially saying it so others could hear how cool you were, fit the expectations of being a "man" during the era. The late sixties definitely were not the conforming 1950's, but being different sexually was still best kept socially quiescent with the closet locked and the key in a safe place.

When Derek became a popular teacher in a public high school, females were paying attention to him for the first time in his twenty-four years. The students realized that Derek was a teacher, but the "forbidden fruit" led some female students who looked for peer approval, or even envy, to spend time with the "cool" teacher.

Even though students may not have found Derek physically attractive, some students found the idea of spending extra time with a teacher exciting and a symbol of status. Friends rewarded flirtatious students with an incredulous "wow." Such admiration among one's peer group can be heady stuff, especially when accompanied by displays of jealousy, or an occasional, "I wish I could do that."

Teachers need to be aware of such things, and a willing Mr. D. in a car in the dark with a student was a serious lack of judgment. It didn't help that a policeman found him in a car with Lydia, albeit an 18-year-old student. Not criminal on the face of it, but not smart either.

In our meeting that cool, damp, rainy April morning after spring break, Derek insisted he was ready and willing to fight for his job. "I have tenure, don't I."

"Yes, you do. But, you should not have been in that car with Lydia. That is what you did wrong. Mitchell wants you out and I must say you should not have fallen for being the 'cool teacher.' It appears as if you acted on your popularity with students. Mitchell suspects 'popular' teachers. Now he has some evidence against you that you have been too popular. Mitchell loathes cool teachers."

I continued, "Mitchell wants you out. When this superintendent wants you out, Derek, you are on your way out. He may not get you on a particular issue but he has notes on all of us. If you used a sick day to go to a Boston Red Sox baseball game and someone saw you there and mentioned your unauthorized absence to Mitchell, then he has recorded the date, time, and who told him. He would have a case against you because you are not supposed to use a sick day to go to a game. He has you, and he has some of the rest of us too if we do something that he really doesn't like. And, Derek, you did go to that Sox game didn't you?"

Without waiting for the answer, I said, "You called in sick. Mitchell most assuredly has a record of that somewhere in his files. This superintendent does not like even a scent of scandal in his school district. Derek, you are cooked. He has you."

Derek had that look on his face that one gets when you know

it is all over and that you've been had. He then asked me, "Do you think I will ever teach again?"

I responded, "Derek, I think you're a great teacher. I hope you do teach again, but I don't know. You have learned a very difficult lesson."

Derek packed his personal belongings in an available trash bag, said "Good bye," then walked out of Bailey High. I covered his first period class. The students asked where he was. I mumbled a few words to distract. I then used Derek's technique of asking questions about the topic of the day which diverted the students. The topic that day was what looked like the approaching end of the American involvement in South Vietnam—the "fall of Saigon."

It was April 1975. By mid-afternoon, Derek had already gathered his goods from his small apartment in town. He was on his way out of Gorham, Massachusetts. Derek did not know where he was going or what awaited him when he got there. He just knew that Mitchell would make sure that this former teacher crossed the town line before the sun set. As was his custom, Derek did what was expected of him. He drove straight ahead.

Chapter 5:
Mark

J received a call from one of my fraternity brothers, "Mark, would you like to go to Woodstock with us? There is going to be a music festival in upstate New York in August. Can you go?"

It was the beginning of the summer of 1969 when Julian called. "Sorry, Julian, but I can't make it. I need to make some money before the fall semester begins. I am waiting on tables at a local restaurant. I really have to buckle down and save some cash before my senior year. So, unfortunately I have to regretfully say no."

At the time of Julian's call, I was planning my final year at the state university. I was majoring in history with little idea of what I was going to do upon graduation.

Immediately after graduating from high school in 1966, I had entered college. I wasn't a great student but I did enough to get by. I didn't party much—some—and I did like to have fun. College was a good place for me to find out how far I wanted to go both academically and socially. I didn't do as much in either my classes or in campus life as I thought I would or wanted to. I was an average student. I floated through the courses I was marginally invested it. I did not overly exert myself in college as I scampered through the four-year experience. I developed skill at dodging the gatekeeping

23

courses. I did just enough to eventually earn my degree.

I played basketball and football in high school. I didn't always have my priorities straight. No one would have called me a "nerd" (a term my students understood and used in describing me as their teacher) or a "brain." I didn't have glasses yet, so I looked more like a jock. I just didn't behave like the stereotype of a jock, which was indeed a stereotype. Some of the smartest people I have known are "jocks."

In college, my friends called me both "a cornball" and "square," or variations of the theme. I guess I was and still am straight-laced. I did not and still do not find it offensive to be called what I am. I have worn some of the name-calling as a badge of honor.

I had always been interested in history and other social sciences, but that was the extent of my academic interests. I spent an inordinate amount of time playing fraternity intramurals in college. After a series of knee and ankle injuries suffered in games, I stopped playing competitive sports. I eventually excelled in games of HORSE where I did not have to overly exert myself.

When my organized sports-playing days ended, I concentrated more on academics in college. I received some A's in my history classes. I earned B's and C's and an occasional D in the rest of my courses. I learned early that if it looked like I would not do well in a course, I could drop it and take another course. Science, math, and languages baffled me. These subjects were not my strong disciplines and I did not discipline myself enough when I took them.

Generally, when I was interested in a subject, I did well. History and the social sciences were my interests so I scored above average in those courses. When I became a teacher, I recommended to students that they follow their interests. If they did, I claimed, "You will do better in school and in life." I further advised my students, "Find out what you love to do, get really good at what you love to do, and then find someone to pay you for it." I added, "The last part is the easiest. Finding what you love to do is the hard part. Once you find your passion, you will never feel like you are working."

I grew up in a town in New Hampshire where there was history all around. The historical preservation people were at it all the time preserving this and that. I did not fully comprehend it when I was growing up, but I grew to eventually understand the value of the history in my home town.

In my youth, the Chamber of Commerce certainly understood the possibility of throngs of window shopping tourists who had money to spend on quaint artifacts in trendy stores. The window shoppers also enjoyed the expensive restaurants that filled the coffers of their owners.

My hometown's store-fronts looked historic even when they had just been remodeled to look like they were from an earlier, more romantic time. The historic architecture of the town made it look stress-free, but there were stresses all around. Some of the town's residents took refuge in its history, never really making it out of the past. The present was too stressful.

When I began college in 1966, a distant place called Vietnam was gaining in importance as additional Americans were going there and many were not coming back. The military draft lurked especially when the conflict escalated. Watching and reading the news each day made it clear that more and more Americans were dying in a country few of us knew anything about.

We didn't know at the time what the Gulf of Tonkin Resolution of 1964 meant, what its implications were, or why the Vietnam conflict mattered. The United States government's rationale was beginning to become apparent— "If we don't stop the Communists in Vietnam, then they would take over all of Southeast Asia"—the so-called "domino effect."

By the mid 1960's, the demonstrations on campus gathered momentum. When I started college, the Tet Offensive in the winter of 1968 was yet to come. Some pundits speculated that Vietnam was a cesspool that the United States could not extricate itself from easily. Most Americans could not see the tragedy about to unfold. As the 1960's progressed, the calamity became more apparent.

Toward the end of the decade, the war seemed to be going nowhere. Too many Americans were coming home in body bags, or were missing in action—never to come home at all. The daily media coverage of the violence inherent in war saturated the three major television networks we had at the time. Bold newspaper headlines reminded us daily about this war in a far off land that few Americans knew about and fewer understood, but more people were caring about daily.

While attending college, I was not one of the demonstrators against the war. I skipped going to Washington, D. C. with some fellow students for the November 1969 protest march. During the march, uniformed police protected the White House. A line of 57 buses shielded the view of the 500,000 protesters crowding Pennsylvania Avenue.

The demonstrators shouted their opposition to the Vietnam War. Because of the cauldron of buses, President Richard M. Nixon and his staff did not have to look out on the unpleasantness. The president and his friends stayed tuned to the Ohio State-Purdue football game. When the volume was turned up high enough, the televised game's noise drowned out the voices of the protesters. The insiders did not have to hear Pete Seeger sing John Lennon's "Give Peace a Chance." When protesters joined in singing the chorus, Seeger asked, an amplified voice above the crowd, "Are you listening, Nixon?" The president was tuned into the game. He was not listening.

In later years, I wish I had gone to Washington to witness the demonstrations, not so much to protest, but to see what was going on. I, like lots of Americans at the time, had not been paying attention but soon would.

The other event I passed on was the Woodstock concert. The happening was a three-hour or so ride from my college campus. Several of my friends and fraternity brothers hitchhiked, car-pooled, or found other ways to make it to rural New York state. I did not go. I later regretted not going because my future students would have valued my first person account of an event relevant to them—a festival of music—with many of the songs protesting against the status quo and the far-away Vietnam conflict that was touching so many souls at home in the late 1960's and early 1970's.

Had I traveled to Woodstock to attend the concert, I may have learned something about the terrain outside New England. I could have met people with opinions different from my own, sometimes radically different. Had I visited places previously unknown, I could have learned more about the world beyond my parochial experience. I could have also observed the emerging counter-culture, which was so alien to my background, my tendencies, and my personal experience. I was and still am a conformist. I am what people usually said of me, "a good boy" who was usually doing what I was told even when what I was told to do was not a good thing to do.

I eventually graduated from college after what seemed like four long years. I was as surprised as anyone else that I actually made it on time to march in the May 1970 commencement. The "on-time" graduation pleased my divorced parents. They each had helped me financially when they could. After the ceremonies, we had a tense family dinner. We did not say much to each other during the five courses, but the silence spoke for us. Upon finishing our dessert, we went our separate ways never to be in the same room at the same time ever again.

My parents had fully experienced the 1960's, whereas I just lived through the decade. I apparently did not "know" the "Sixties" the way my parents did. My parents' long hair and hippie appearance fit in with some of the crowd at the graduation—it was the Zeitgeist of the time. They carved conversations with the filler, "Cool—Man—Cool."

Shortly before I left for college, my parents asked me to call them Momma and Poppa rather than the more traditional "mom" and "pop" that I had previously called them since I could talk. I thought little of it at the time. It seemed to be a strange request but I generally did what my parents told me to do. By the time I was in high school, my parents had divorced and moved to different locations. They never quite made it out of the 1960's.

I did not know any of my grandparents, or anything about them except that they lived and died in Canada. It was all very secretive. I did not understand why it was so furtive and sub rosa. I swore to myself that my children would know their grandparents or at least know about them as people. I missed not knowing mine. I wanted to learn my family's history. I was also getting to the point where I wanted to learn about everything.

Chapter 6:
Ana

*E*xcept for an occasional trip to games or sporting events with my parents or friends, I had seldom been anywhere outside of Maine, Massachusetts or New Hampshire. After graduating from the university, I planned to travel through the parts of the United States I had time and money for. It was the latter part of May, 1970.

I had always been a college football fan, so during my trip I stopped in Austin, Texas, for a night to get the feel of a college community which was host to a perennial college football power, the University of Texas.

In order to save the little money I had, I counted on using my sleeping bag on the streets. The ubiquitous counter-culture, wandering inhabitants and street people of the late 1960's, was generally stonily peaceful. They flopped and slept anywhere they could find a quasi-comfortable spot. The city appeared to allow it as long as there was no trouble. So, I figured that it would be relatively safe to sleep on a sidewalk with self-avowed, peace-loving hippies. Besides, I was short on funds for hotel stays. I liked to eat so I used whatever money I could spare for food. While in Austin, I never made it to the street.

In college, I did not drink a lot but did drink during some social occasions. I enjoyed going out with friends for a beer or two, or three now and then. I did join a fraternity and attended some of the parties. I did not like to be "out of it and out of control"; consequently, my drunken stupors were relatively infrequent. In Austin, much to my surprise, my search for a cheap beer or two led me to Ana.

I had dated some in college but did not go to Texas to find a life-long love or anything like it. I am irredeemably sappy and saccharine about relationships. I admit it. I figured that someday I would find the one and only one. I dreamed hopelessly idyllic thoughts.

I met Ana at a local college hangout in Austin. There was something about her that drew me. I had never seen anyone so enchantingly beautiful. Ana mixed races into a gorgeous human mosaic. As I learned later, her father was from Texas of Latin and African American heritage. Ana's mother was from southern California. Her mother's father was Japanese and her mother was originally from Mexico. Ana's union of her father's and her mother's blended cultures nurtured stunning beauty.

I was enthralled immediately. And, as I found out later, Ana was too. We hit it off right away. It may sound corny, but it was "love at first sight." Maybe because we thought time was short, we did not want to leave much unsaid or hold anything back. We must have thought that our conversation would be left in a bar in Austin.

In our intense discussion, Ana told me, "I never knew or even met my father. My mother got involved with a man she barely knew. I understand how it could happen. I guess. It led to my mother becoming pregnant, even though she knew my father for just a short time. I don't blame the father I never knew nor do I fault my mother for what was essentially a one-night stand. I don't condemn either of them at all."

After a pause and some tears, Ana added, "It just happened."

"Growing up, I lived with my mother. My father was not in my life and that left a void in my heart. I regret never having met or talked with him. I want to find him some day. I want to hug him—hug him tight to make up for some of those years when we did not hold each other. I do not know his name or where he is and my mother will not tell me.

"My mother does not think I need to know who my father is. But, Mark, I believe I am old enough and mature enough. And, I definitely want to know. It irritates me that my mother will not tell me. I have been pretty persistent in asking my mother about my dad and what happened between the two of them."

With her voice drifting off, Ana struggled through the words, "But my mother won't tell me."

Ana continued, "My mother has a stubborn streak. She will not tell me anything about my father or much at all about her own background. If I keep asking her, she just shuts me out. Her silence about him and her really hurts me and makes me mad."

Ana knew her father was black. Her blended heritage was impossible for her to hide, nor did she want to. It was clear to me from the outset that Ana badly wanted to know more about her ancestry—a lot more. She wanted her mother to tell her who her father is and what she knows about him. Ana said, "I will then take care of finding out the rest."

"I want my mother to tell me who he is, how they met, and what happened after their night together. I don't need to have details on that night, but I do really want to know more about my father other than his parentage. I won't tell my mother this because she really wouldn't tell me if she knew, but once I know his name then I will go find him. She wouldn't want me to do that but I would." I don't know why, but at that moment for some reason, I needed her as much as she seemed to need me.

Ana and I talked and talked, getting physically closer with

each word, until we were touching. I had never felt anything like this. It wasn't the beer—it was her—enchanting. We flew with the time until we heard, "Last call."

Ana asked, "Where are you staying?"

"I have a trusty sleeping bag" I said. "I know of a neighborhood that looks safe so I plan to go there to crash with some other transients." Her face filled with incredulity.

Ana paused as she thought about it, responding hesitantly, "I and some friends are in a chorus competition. We are staying in a house where we are all just crashing. Mark, that is your real name isn't it?"

"Yes, it is. Mark Blenchard to be exact." I said as if I were revealing some kind of secret.

"You are welcome to stay with us. Other people are crashing there too. I am sure it is okay."

I didn't have to think about it long before I said, "Yes, I would like to do that. Thanks for the offer. I will be less lonely and have a roof over my head. Wow."

Ana chuckled as she said, "Great, Mark, let's go."

We left the bar and took the short walk to the house Ana's group had rented. When we arrived, we found most of the chorus members asleep. Ana said, "We can have the closet," which was just big enough for the two of us. I began to wonder what in the world was going on. Not only had I never been with a woman before—I had never slept in close proximity to one. Now, I was invited to do so. Slow, sustained anxiety swept through my nerves.

I had girl friends in high school and dated in college. My fraternity brothers considered me to be a "straight Joe" who for the most part stayed out of trouble. I wasn't a prude, but I was what my brothers said about me, "Mark is lost in romanticism." Their laughter invariably followed. Then, "Maybe he is irretrievably lost." Indeed, I did imagine one true love, one day, not now.

I realize I was more puritanical than some others my age, but that was me. When my friends called me "square" or that I am "straight-laced" it didn't bother me. I missed the "sexual revolution" of the 1960's, but I did not care. I would be searching for the right person to spend the rest of my life with. Old-fashioned, I know. Although, the search was a future aspiration. I was not looking during my present journey; I was not ready. Or, at least I didn't think I was.

So, when I was about to share a space for a night with a woman, it was the closest I had ever come to sharing a room— or closet— with a female for a night. It seemed awkward, but in a way it didn't. My nervous system settled into spasms.

I found the bathroom, brushed my teeth, and washed. Ana followed when I was done. It seemed like an eternity waiting for Ana to come out. When she came out in pajamas, I averted my gaze. I just could not look at her as she slipped into the make-shift bed.

I usually slept in my underwear, but tonight I put on a t-shirt and sweatpants. My flooded nerves surged again into a steady panic. I had clothes on but felt naked. After another bathroom visit, I dropped down next to Ana. We had enough room on the floor so we did not have to touch unless we wanted to. But we did want to touch. We soon touched, and touched, and touched. I had never had full intercourse with a woman although in college I had played and petted to climax. If IT was going to happen, it was because it was meant to be. I couldn't explain it logically nor was I about to try. I just went with it, whatever IT was. I was losing the control I had always tried to keep.

The hot, humid Texas air on this late May night turned steamy. The air conditioning was not fully functioning, so already dripping with perspiration we slowly removed some of our clothing. I don't know why, but when I touched her, the heat of her body just drove me out of my life-long, rational, logic-locked-mind. As the heat of the evening and Ana's body made my sweat glands secrete uncontrollably, the strangeness of what was happening that evening multiplied. I had never done anything or felt anything like this before.

I couldn't tell whether what was occurring was right or wrong. I decided even if it wasn't right— it was happening—I just went with it. My "be in control at all times and be reasonable" tendencies were still trying to get in the way of where I wanted to go emotionally and physically. For one of the first times in my life, I let go. My brain frizzled.

After we removed the rest of each other's clothing, Ana and I were making love. She fit into me, and I into her—all seemed right with the world. I exploded quickly and settled into the moist warmth of Ana's body. I was limp and embarrassed. What had I done? A flurry of insecurities raced through me. What now?

Ana said all of the right things to comfort me because I thought I had come too fast and had not pleased her. She said, "Mark, it was wonderful, just right." I was not quite sure whether to believe her or not, but for the next two hours we hugged and stroked each other. Her touch was tender—her skin soft and smooth. The cares of the world mattered not at that moment.

We eventually fell to sleep in each other's arms. We woke when light fluttered into a hallway where a curtain had not been closed. To get air circulating on a humid night, we had left the door cracked. Light shimmered at daybreak.

It was 7:30 a.m., chorus members rushed to have breakfast so they could digest as they rehearsed for a 10 a.m. performance. I begged off on having breakfast because everyone was moving at a crisper pace than I was or wanted to after the nervy bliss I felt just hours before. I didn't want it all to evaporate although I feared it would. I started to wonder whether we had done the right thing as Mark began to get in the way of Mark.

Ana and I exchanged phone numbers and addresses. I did not know if I would ever see her again. We parted with uncomfortable goodbyes. I went to a bakery for coffee and a bagel. Ana readied for her competition. Our last words to each other were "See ya, Ana," and, "See ya, Mark." The old "Seeyas" where you realized you may never see each other again.

After breakfast, I went to the post office and checked in general delivery to see if I had any mail waiting for me. I had planned to stop in Austin, so arranged for mail to be sent there. A bill for $49 had followed me to Texas. There was also a letter from my mother.

Chapter 7:
Momma

My mother had dwelled in distress for years after the divorce from my father. Even though it occurred a long time ago, the separation and divorce still bothered her. I think there was still some addictive attraction between them.

In the letter I received in Texas, my mother asked, "Mark, could you please come home to see me and be with me as soon as you return?" She seldom asked me to come see her. Yet, this request had the sense of urgency. She did not provide an explanation, so I speculated something must be up that I needed to attend to.

I had already explored more geography outside New England than I ever had in my life. After hearing from my mother, I turned around. I boarded a bus and left Texas and Ana behind. I headed to my mother's apartment in Massachusetts to see why she wanted me to come home to see her.

When I arrived at my mother's house, she said even before we had exchanged hellos, "I have something to tell you." Without any preliminaries, she said, "I have cancer. It is terminal. I may not have long to live." The rest of the visit did not get any easier.

My mother had worked odd jobs before she met my father.

When they met, she was bartending at a local club. They hit it off and married six months later. I came along six months after that and we moved to a rental in New Hampshire.

My father worked as a salesman, but never for very long in any one job. When I was four or five years old their fighting intensified. He began to spend nights away from home and eventually they called it quits. He went off to do his "Sixties" thing. My mother tried to make ends meet and save some money so I could go to college. Even though it was not easy for her, Momma's help enabled me to get a degree. Now she had cancer!

After spending several weeks with my mother. I realized that I needed to find a job. Maybe I could even help my mother if I had some money coming in.

My history major in college provided some knowledge, but I believed that I had few marketable skills. I didn't realize then, until I started teaching, that my history degree could be valuable in a number of professions. Once I started teaching, I understood the value of studying history. I communicated the economic and intellectual value of knowing history to my skeptical students, some of whom eventually bought into the concept and majored or minored in history in college.

I had taken some education courses, so substitute teaching was a possibility as a starter. After substituting for a while, I figured I could find a job in another profession that carried a larger salary and more prestige.

After I had somewhat settled my mother's fears and uneasiness, and I thought she might be okay for a while, I went to the local school system's main office.

It was now the beginning of August 1970, so I thought the local school system might be looking for possible substitute teachers with school beginning in September. I went to the system's administration offices, opened the door, introduced myself, and asked the receptionist, "How should I go about applying for a substitute teaching position?"

Without answering my question, she directed me to "Please take a seat Mr. Blenchard. The superintendent is out of town and cannot be contacted, but the assistant superintendent will be with you shortly."

The school system contained one high school, a junior high school, and three elementary schools. I thought that I might be able to handle substituting in junior high and high school in history and social studies courses.

After a few minutes, the receptionist guided me in to the assistant superintendent's office. The assistant superintendent, a woman maybe in her late 50's, fit the stereotype of an educator prior to 1900: granny glasses, two inch heels, and clothes that hid anything that could possibly stimulate the young.

We exchanged pleasantries, and then she said "So, you are looking for a job?"

I couldn't tell whether it was a question or a command. I responded, "Yes, I am."

"You may be in luck young man. We just had a resignation and we need a full time high school history teacher. Orientation sessions start in three weeks. Do you think you could teach high school history and social studies here in Gorham and be ready to start when school begins?"

Without much thought about what I was getting into, I said, "Yes." I needed a job and she appeared to be offering one. The rest of the interview was what I was to learn was the modus operandi for job interviews—the interviewer talked and the interviewee listened.

I left the assistant superintendent's office and asked the receptionist for the necessary paperwork to get hired. I completed the application.

I did not have pay phone money with me, so I inquired if

there was a phone I could use to call the university to request a transcript. "Yes, Mr. Blenchard, there's a phone over there next to the bookcase that you can use for that purpose."

The receptionist continued, "The transcript and three letters of recommendation should be sent to the assistant superintendent. If everything comes in and the recommendations are alright, you will begin teaching right after Labor Day." In an hour and 15 minutes I had become a teacher.

As I left the school system's building. I wasn't sure whether to be happy or petrified. I really did not know very much about teaching but it was a job and I might as well give it a try. Besides, I mused, how difficult could it be?

I hadn't checked my mail for a while in part because I expected to hear from a bill collector. So, with some apprehension, I went down to the local post office which collected the mail that I did not have redirected. I had no fixed address, so I had mail sent to general delivery in the various towns I would be in for a day or two. That way I could check for mail when I was brave enough to do so, or anticipated receiving something I actually wanted to get.

When I arrived at my home post office, I did, indeed, receive mail from a bill collector indicating that I now owed $64 because interest had accumulated and would be accumulating daily.

Another letter was waiting for me. It was from Ana. I opened it before determining what I needed to do with the bill.

"Dear Mark, I hesitated to write to you. I thought for a long time not doing so, but I thought that I must for both you and me. I have missed my monthly two times in a row. I realize we did not know each other very well when we met that night in Austin, so I would fully understand if I never see you again, but I thought I should let you know. I am Catholic and will have the baby.

With regards and love for that special night in Austin, Ana."

I dashed off a response, "Ana, I am coming down to be with you.

Love, Mark."

I put my eleven words in the mail box to the return address as fast as I could. I wanted to get my response to Ana as soon as possible, because I was going to be with her. I had enough money to buy a bus ticket to Texas, and if Ana would return with me I had some things I could pawn to obtain enough money for both Ana and me to return to Massachusetts. I tucked some clothes into a travel bag. I caught a bus at 9 p.m. I was on my way.

After a bus trip that seemed to take forever, I arrived in Texas. I found a pay phone. I hurriedly called the phone number Ana had given me when we said goodbye that May day in Austin. Someone answered. I asked, "Is Ana there?"

I could hear the person I reached say, "Somebody is calling for you Ana."

Without asking who it was, Ana took the phone.

"Hello. Is this you Ana?" Without waiting for a response, I hastily said, "Ana, its Mark, I will be right there."

I did not even give her time to respond. I asked a bystander for directions and ran with my bag the mile to where she was staying. I knocked on the door. Ana opened it. She looked as beautiful—more so—than she did that night more than two months ago.

In 1970, if a pregnancy occurred, marriage was the usual course of action. I was not going to let Ana experience this alone, besides it was OUR baby. And, like Ana, aborting a baby was not an option for me either. We were going to have our baby, and I was determined we were going to do it together.

As soon as I saw her, I asked her, "Will you marry me? Will

you come home with me?"

She looked at me stunned. Her look of surprise verged on shock. Without thinking about the proposal any more than I had in making it, Ana said, "Yes."

After we recovered from a whirl of elation-filled tears, Ana said, "I will call my mother."

Ana's mother was difficult to reach because she had to use the phone of a friend. Later that day, her mother called back. More tears were shed. I got the gist of the conversation. It was clearly painful for both of them. Ana's mother broke off the call before much could be said and hung up. Ana cried uncontrollably. Anguish spread through her. I tried to comfort her but at the moment nothing could.

Later that evening, I convinced her that even without her mother's approval the sooner we got married the better. Then we would at least have each other. My romanticism had kicked in without a scintilla of forethought about what we might face in the future.

We decided to get a marriage license the next day. After a brief waiting period, we arranged a noon ceremony. In a plain, non-descript, yet sun-lit office, a Justice of the Peace married us on August 15, 1970. The Justice of the Peace's wife and an assistant witnessed our union as husband and wife. No one else was there except our son.

On the afternoon of our wedding, we boarded a bus to go to Massachusetts and find an apartment. I was about to start a new job in a profession that I knew precious little about.

Ana and I did not have a honeymoon, or anything resembling one. For better or worse, Ana and I were married. We would have to see if one night of impulsive, balmy intimacy would lead to a life filled with love.

"Did our marriage even have a chance to last?" I asked myself, afraid of telling Ana what I was thinking: "Could it?

Would it? Should it?"

Under the circumstances, I wondered whether we could possibly make it work in the long run. I had asked Ana to come home with me although I had no home. But, I thought, together we could find a way to make a home for us and our baby.

I looked at Ana and knew that even though we had known each other such a brief time that we had to give it a try, and even though it was a "one night stand," that we might be able to make it work. I believed, maybe foolishly, that I loved her and would forever. I hoped she loved me, or someday would.

We had no money. We had no place to live. We decided to name our baby Joel or Suzie.

Chapter 8:
Mom

*A*na and I talked a lot during the pregnancy about our relationship. We both seemed sure it would survive, although we had no evidence that it would after such a brief encounter. Many marriages fail, especially those of couples who knew little of each other before saying "I do." We were expecting a baby to boot with little money to buy the boots.

Talking it through seemed to help. Young and innocent as we were we believed that love would conquer all. Maybe it would. We would have to see if the fairy tale comes true.

We talked about Ana's mother frequently. She seemed to always be on Ana's mind. "Mom moves around a lot," Ana said.

"Is there any particular reason for that?" I asked.

"Yes. She works with migrant workers mainly on the west coast. Mom is a midwife, so she delivers and cares for babies. She can also take care of injuries of which there are many among the workers. Workers and their families do not have money for regular doctors or hospitals. Mom takes care of men, women and children. My mother can bring a baby to life, take care of snake bites, and even sew back salvageable severed fingers and toes. Migrants cannot afford expensive medical care, or in most cases any medical care at all. So, my Mom is the care-giver. Mom is it for them. Mom and others like her.

The migrant families depend on my Mom and others who can help to provide at least minimal care. Without them, migrants have no care beyond each other."

"Ana, until I read about it recently, I must admit that I had little idea of what was going on in the fields. What happens to migrant workers is what we read about in 'third world' reports. I wonder if American citizens know about the fate of these people. I wonder if our society cares. It is as if these are invisible people."

"Yes, Mark, the migrant workers and their families are unseen and ignored. Mom is very concerned about the rights of workers. She believes the owners of the fields push around and exploit the workers. Not only do many of the migrants live in squalid and unhealthy circumstances, they have very little power to get jobs that pay more money or to better their living conditions. Politicians like to call it capitalism at work, but it is more like piece-work peonage."

"This does not sound like the good old U. S. A. to me."

"It isn't, Mark. It is another world—different from the one most Americans live in."

"When you were young, did you move around with your mother, or did you stay with relatives?"

"I traveled with Mom. I had very little formal schooling. I did learn to read. I learned to love reading and still do. In the camps, we would get together at night around a campfire and tell stories. Those workers who could read taught us how to read. After the campfire stories, and before we went to sleep at night, we would read to each other. So, I learned to love reading. Books were my education. We didn't have many, so I read some of them over and over again. Some of the other children were not so lucky and never learned how to read. It is hard to love books when you cannot read them."

"It sounds like your mother is a fascinating person who has

been doing important work. Please tell me more Ana."

"My mother had always fought for the rights of migrant workers in California. She still is fighting. I am never sure where she is. She has a friend I call who is able to get a message to her."

"Did you have any formal education at all?"

"Some. I would start a grade in September, but never finish because we moved so often. My education was really sporadic, but I picked things up. I did not attend kindergarten. I missed not being a kindergartener the most. In some of the towns we went through, I would see kids playing in school playgrounds. I badly wanted to join them. But I never did. We were always on the move from one field to another. There were no playgrounds where we worked. I started working in the fields as soon as I was old enough."

"How old was that?"

"When I reached double figures—10 years old."

"Were you allowed to work that young? What about child labor laws?"

Ana smiled as if she understood my naiveté. "Mark, they might as well have been non-existent in the fields. Without a union representative to inform us and intervene for us, we did not know about the laws. If there were such laws, they were not enforced. We worked from dawn to dusk. There was no time for school."

"What did you and your mother do in the camps as you went from one camp to another?"

"When I wasn't working, I would accompany her while she delivered babies. The babies became children, did not attend school very much if at all, and they eventually went to work. When they were considered old enough, they picked fruits and vegetables in the fields."

"At what age were the children old enough to work the

fields?"

"Well, it depended on the child. Some went to work before they were ten. Others went to work later—but usually not much later. As I mentioned, I went to work at 10 which was about average."

"If the labor laws didn't help, how about the compulsory school laws? Didn't state requirements to attend educational institutions apply?"

"No, Mark, you are way too innocent to the ways of the 'make as much profit as you can' work world. Many of these kids were not citizens of the United States, and moved around a lot. In many cases, there were no official birth certificates. In a way, migrant workers did not exist except to pick food and other products for the nation's dinner tables and restaurants. I and my fellow migrant workers were, for all intents and purposes, pawns in the larger society. As long as the food got to people's tables, we weren't given a second thought. The compulsory school laws were unenforceable in large part because the owners of the fields influenced the school boards and the city councils in the various towns. So, there was no appealing to a higher authority."

"And your mother was trying to take care of these folks as best she could?"

"Yes, and I have no idea where she is now. But with our baby coming, I have to reach her. It will be her first grandbaby. She has to know."

Ana attended some public school classes along the way, but never completely finished a grade. She earned her high school equivalency, and was accepted to a state college where she majored in education. When I met her in Texas, in May of 1970, she was with her college chorus on a trip after her freshman year. Shortly after we got married, Ana dropped out of college. A couple of friends wondered why she left town so quickly with a man she hardly knew. Only Ana's mother knew she was pregnant.

Our baby was due on February 22, 1971. As the due date approached, it looked as if the predicted date would hold. It was becoming clear that the birth was not going to be without complications. The pregnancy had been a difficult one. When the time came, I would have to get her to the hospital fast and hope that they knew what to do with a pregnancy that had not gone smoothly. The hospital staff had assured us that they could take care of Ana and our baby.

On February 21st, we heard a knock on our apartment door where we lived at the time in Gorham, Massachusetts. Ana opened it and there she was— her mother. Ana screamed "Mom!"

I was in our bedroom when I heard Ana scream. Not knowing what was going on and afraid that the baby might be coming immediately, I hurried into the room that served as a dining room, kitchen, and living room. After I saw that our baby had not suddenly appeared, I realized that someone had come into the house. As soon as I recognized danger had not entered the house, I meekly said "Hello" to the person who had come in. Still wondering who this was coming to our door that caused Ana to scream, I plopped onto the couch. Questions surged through me but I just sat—jaw agape.

I could barely talk as I began to recognize who must have come in. I mumbled something like "Um." Ana recovered as soon as she saw her astonished husband and calmly introduced me to my mother-in-law. "Mark, this is my mother—your mother-in-law."

I managed to eke out a "Hello. It is nice to meet you."

Ana, as stunned as I was, asked, "Mom, what are you doing here?"

"I came to take care of my daughter and deliver my

49

grandbaby," her mother said with conviction. It was clear that she had made up her mind that was exactly what she was going to do and wasn't about to accept a "No you're not." It did not take me long to figure out that when Ana's mother made up her mind that denying her was not in the equation.

I had little idea what was going on and what "Mom" planned to do, but was assured through the sound of her voice that she meant what she said and knew what she was doing.

"Welcome into our home." I said. "What should I call you?"

"Just call me Mom" she said.

"Henceforth, Mom it is. I am pleased to meet you."

Ana and her mother embraced for a long time. I then hugged her mother in my usual obligatory hug. I still didn't know what was happening.

Mom had worked as a migrant worker as a child, and continued that work into adulthood. She never attended school. By candle light in the camps, she learned how to read with the help of the workers and other children. Her father and mother died before she was five. A family working in the fields took care of her until her thirteenth birthday when she was on her own. Ana was born when her mother was eighteen. By the time I met Mom, the sun had burned wrinkles into her skin making her look older than she must have been. I did not ask.

We did not have any medical insurance, so we had wondered how we were going to pay for the delivery and the hospital. We had pieced together enough money to pay for the necessary care during the pregnancy. I was ready to do what was required to take care of my wife and our baby. I was afraid that it might be a complicated delivery, and I did not want to take any chances. I planned to borrow the money necessary to take care of my wife and baby.

Before I could say anything further, Mom declared, "I will deliver the baby here. You can help Mark. I am not going to have someone else birthing my grandbaby."

Ana explained, "Mom is a certified midwife and has delivered many babies. Why not birth the baby the old-fashioned way—in our apartment. Mom can use what we have in the house to deliver the baby. She has brought to life so many babies in places where there was nothing available. Anything we absolutely need, we can get at the pharmacy."

By now, Ana could see in my expression that I needed more assurance. "Mark, Mom has delivered a lot of healthy babies among farm workers in the fields of California in much worse conditions than our apartment. She knows what to do. It will be okay. Okay? Mark, it really will be alright."

We didn't have a lot of choices. With no insurance and little available money, I agreed that Mom could deliver the baby in our home. I would have to get over my own squeamishness fast. Ana had convinced me that Mom could deliver our baby safely.

Mom had already told us that she had to return to California as soon as she could for her job working with farm workers in the fields of southern California. The problem was that Ana might not deliver as scheduled. Mom said, "Ana, will deliver soon. I calculated from the day she told me and when she must have conceived. Mark, it will be soon. I promise you. I know my daughter."

Indeed, Mom was going to stay to make sure her grandchild was born, and that her daughter and grandchild were in good health. Then Mom could and would go.

After conversation late into the night, we went to bed. Ana said she was not feeling anything. At 4 A.M. on February 22nd, Ana's water broke. She was feeling our baby now.

Mom seemed to have a sixth sense about things and was washed and ready when I went to find her on the couch. I had offered her the bed with Ana, but she explained that after sleeping on bare floors and open ground for so many nights she found the prospect of a couch a luxury.

Mom delivered Joel at 6:27 a.m. on February 22, 1971. Joel weighed in at 6 pounds 8 ounces. It was a complicated pregnancy but not a complicated delivery. Mom joyfully lifted her arms with Joel in her hands as she presented her grandbaby to the world.

After Joel was born, Mom and Ana sat together with the baby on the couch as they caressed each other and our new born son. Mom said she had to leave that afternoon to return to Texas. She had been willing to stay longer to see her grandson born, but that staying any longer would have been pushing it. Now that she had this time with Ana and had brought forth her grandson she felt she could and should return to her life's work.

Mom gave us instructions on how to care for our baby in the coming weeks. "Mark and Ana, if you follow these steps, Joel will be on his way to a healthy and happy beginning. I know he will."

Mom was going back to Texas to meet with farm workers who were preparing to join Cesar Chavez in California in protest of the treatment of migrant workers in that state. Chavez stirred controversy wherever he went. Mom relished the controversy and challenges that were ahead of her. As she was about to leave our home, Mom said, "I am proud to march with Cesar."

I planned to drive Mom to the bus station, but when it came time Mom said, "No Mark. You must stay with Ana and Joel. I have saved my pennies for a taxi, so please call a cab."

We called a taxicab to bring Mom to the bus station in the next town. The tears flowed as we said our goodbyes. She had delivered and embraced her grandson. We all hoped that she would see him again soon. As she was entering the taxi, she said something as if we should know what she was talking about but we did not understand. "I will tell Danny. He will want to know."

We had no idea who Danny was, but we were anxious to find out. We did not know whether he was a friend, partner, fellow worker, or relative. The taxi drove off with Mom before we could ask about his identity.

On a cold, snowy winter day in February, Mom left to return to her work in the fields. Ana and I hoped Mom's spirit would always reside in our son because of those birth hours Mom spent with Joel.

I had also hoped that my mother would get to know my children. Shortly after Ana and I arrived in New England, it was apparent to both of us that my mother did not have long to live. She died on December 26, 1970.

Momma knew that Ana and I were going to have a baby. We spent Christmas day with her. She was cognizant enough to feel Ana's belly in search of her grandchild. Before she died on the next day, she thought she touched Joel.

After Joel was born in February of 1971, I tried to reach my father to notify him of the birth of his grandson. I never did reach him.

Chapter 9:
Joel and Suzie

*O*ur son, Joel, was born eight months and two weeks after Ana and I first met on that star-filled Texas evening. Suzie blessed us two years later. Because of difficult pregnancies and for financial reasons, we decided that we would stop at two children.

Shortly after Suzie's birth in the summer of 1973, I became the chair of the social studies department at Bailey T. S. Memorial High School, which along with being an assistant basketball coach for a couple of years, brought in a little extra money. Ana finished her final year of college at night at a local university's extension service. Through taking night courses, she gradually earned her college degree and became certified to teach kindergarten through second grade.

Ana started teaching in one of the elementary schools in our district six months after Suzie was born. With growing children, we believed we needed the second income. Suzie spent her pre-school years in a neighborhood day care center. Joel started pre-kindergarten when he was four.

After Suzie's birth, Ana worried about her weight. I, too, had a weight problem. At six feet two inches, I had played basketball in high school. I also played tight end for my high school football team. I was too slow to make the football team in college, and not tall enough to play forward on the basketball team. When I stopped playing organized sports, I went from one hundred eighty pounds in my senior year of high school to well over two hundred before entering college. Both Ana and I worked to control our weight, which for me was a losing battle.

In college I seldom worked out. I gained more than the alleged "freshman fifteen" pounds, growing to almost two hundred and thirty-five pounds by the end of my freshman year in college. I spent a lot of time in the dining hall. I added more pounds to my already substantial frame by graduation day.

I began a walking regimen to at least maintain my weight and not gain more. I hoped to lose some of the extra pounds. My attempts at losing weight were not successful. I liked to eat and walking just helped me to keep from gaining still more weight.

Ana, five feet two inches in height, weighed one hundred and twenty pounds when we got married. She told me that after carrying two children, "I have gained weight carrying both Joel and Suzie. I worry about it. I am still gaining weight Mark. What should I do about it?"

I repeatedly told her, "As long as you feel healthy, Ana, I would not be concerned. You look beautiful to me. I love you so."

Ana responded to my "You look beautiful to me" comment with a look of incredulity. I think she wanted to believe me, but often didn't see the beauty in herself. In my eyes, her beauty was there for the entire world to see.

Before Ana started teaching, the only exercise she got was playing with Joel and Suzie. Once she started teaching, she moved around and played as much as she could with her kindergarteners. I realized it sounded "corny" when I told her over and over that she was "still beautiful to me." But that was me. "I love you the way you are." I told her. I meant it.

Shortly after I became chair of the social studies

department, Ana and I decided to invite some teachers from Bailey High for occasional Friday night potluck dinners in our home. This would give us all a chance to get to know each other, talk about our lives and teaching, discuss school and national issues, and spend some informal time together.

We decided, at least at first, to invite teachers from the high school. The invitees would mainly be from the social studies department but not exclusively. We hoped to invite new colleagues as time went on. Our district's school population was growing and we would need to add more teachers to the district's staff. Ana wanted to invite one or two of her elementary school colleagues to the potlucks once she got to know teachers in her school better.

For the first potluck, we invited social studies teachers Ken Lewiston, Megan Straffa, Jake Spanner, Charles Yates, and Derek Randallston, who was still teaching in the social studies department at the time. We also asked Karla Betts, an art teacher, and Cheryl Wattsen who teaches English to join us. All agreed to attend. With Ana and me, we had a comfortable group of nine.

Our first Friday potluck was held toward the end of October, 1973. We had some national news to discuss. We wanted to discuss how to teach about "The Saturday Night Massacre" come Monday.

Chapter 10:
Megan

The students fathomed Ms. M. a mystery. When their courage was up, and they thought I would not ignore them or bristle at their inquiries about Ms. M., one student after another would ask about her, "What's up with Ms. M.?"

Others chimed in, "Yeah, what's up with her?" The students were incessantly curious about Ms. M.

Megan Straffa joined the social studies faculty at the same time I did in the fall of 1970. I never got to know her well although we talked frequently. Megan was not an easy person to know, although you might think you knew her. I don't think anyone really did.

As a faculty, we knew about Megan, but did not really know Megan. Megan's personality lacked even a tinge of subtlety. Yet, she seemed unknowable, even incomprehensible. Maybe the students had it right—mysterious. They also called her "Power Woman." An appellation I could not completely understand, but her students did.

Megan graduated from a private liberal arts university. She majored in history while double minoring in philosophy and English. She then earned a master's degree in education at a state university before she started to teach.

Ms. M. perplexed her students in part because she was so

different from anyone they had previously encountered. Her students thought of her as weird at first but got used to Ms. M.'s "strange ways." They concluded that she was just odd, and that maybe being distinct wasn't all bad. I thought—a good lesson to learn.

In one of our conversations, Megan said, "I did not know my father. My mother and I lived alone. We both had a string of odd jobs so we could pay the bills."

I responded, "I can relate to that. My wife, Ana, never knew her father either and feels it to this day. She and her mother had to thread a living together also. So, I think I understand."

Megan said further, "As soon as I was old enough, I worked twenty to thirty hours a week until I went to college. I then worked forty hours a week while attending the university until I earned my degree. I worked as a waitress, custodial work, anything to make a buck."

Work Megan knew how to do. She did it all the time, and did it well. She seemed to be compulsively busy, almost as if slowing down would be sacrilegious. I never fully appreciated or grasped the perpetual motion that was Megan. I watched incredulously as she moved and kept moving. Some people sip through life—Megan guzzled.

I asked Megan about her whirlwind work habits and how she stayed so slender. She seemed to be snacking all the time and I seldom if ever saw her exercise. "Work, work, work. Nervous energy, Mark. That's all. No secret diet or exercise program. I am going at it all the time. Go, Go, Go. Got to eat though. It keeps me going. Fuel for the body. You know. You should move more Mark. You could lose some weight and maybe you would live longer."

I did not want to get too personal, although she had given me entry by referring to my body size, so I asked her, "How about relaxing Megan, don't you relax some time?"

"No, no time. Too many things to do. Too much to accomplish. No time to just sit down. Except…maybe…to eat." She let out a laugh at the last thought.

"I don't have any brothers or sisters that I know about," Megan said with a smirk. "I suppose there might be other family members. My mother never married, but had been in and out of relationships. I may have a sibling or two or maybe more. Though I don't know," Megan added in a resigned off-handed manner.

"When I was a toddler," Megan explained, "My mother would periodically leave me in the care of a friend or relative while my mother left for anywhere from a couple of days to a week or so."

Megan, while still moving—never sitting down, also told me, "My mother and I have never talked about the past. Even when I was old enough and willing to understand, she avoided the subject whenever I brought it up. When I persisted, my mother would throw a guilt trip at me."

Megan was able to repeat her mother's oral venom verbatim, "Megan, get the fuck off my case. You upset me when you ask me about those things you little bitch. Leave me alone and mind your own damned business. You ungrateful brat. I feed you and put a roof over your fucking head don't I. Just shut the fuck up."

Megan's emotional rendition of her mother's hurtful words made it clear that the toxicity did, indeed, injure. But her mother was the only one she had—the only person she seemed to be close to. And there did not seem to be any other woman or, for that matter, man in her life. She never spoke to me about a relative or anyone else that might be close to her. I didn't ask either.

Megan reported that her high school experience was uneventful. She conveyed to me, "I was not a joiner and never what you would call popular." Megan seemed to have a pretty good understanding of who she was, and who she was not. She just didn't seem to want to let anyone else in through her snug façade.

She went further, "I did well enough in high school to earn a merit scholarship to a selective college where I continued to pretty much stay to myself. It didn't ever enter my mind to join a sorority."

Megan satirized the "beauty culture" of the campus "meat market" as she put it. Megan did not try to look any special way for anyone—including herself. Even while in college, Megan exhorted political and social causes. Her priorities were those issues that she believed mattered to the welfare of people and the social change necessary to help people live better lives. Megan employed the terminology "social justice" before it was in vogue to do so. Megan relished her own non-conformity.

While studying in one of her minors, English, she read widely even when it was not required. She especially read women authors. Megan cited authors Mary Wollstonecraft, Gabriela Mistral and Betty Friedan frequently. She recommended that we all read Maya Angelou's, Nikki Giovanni's and Toni Morrison's writings, as well as Phillis Wheatley's early American poetry. This drove some of her students and colleagues wild—often to distraction. Others read what Megan recommended.

In the early 1970's, the women's movement gained traction. Courses in women's studies, although still in their infancy, were growing. Some students and faculty wondered what women meant by liberation. Megan declared, "You should find out." She iced ignorance.

I tend to be conciliatory in arguments. Megan challenged me and put me on the defensive. She had the ability to get under my skin. She insisted repeatedly that I really did not get it.

"Mark, you seem to be a nice guy but you have no idea what women go through."

"What do you mean?" I tried to defend myself. "I think I understand. Give me a break."

"Mark, damn it, you would have to live in our shoes. You guys leering at women all the time like we are inanimate objects. Men are more interested in our bodies than our brains. Men are intent on getting us in bed rather than talking about issues with us. After a while, it gets really tiresome. All you guys want is a quick screw— 'bam-bam, thank you ma'am'— then you are off to the next conquest. I know this is an over-generalization. But, Mark, you get the idea don't you?"

"Keep going, Megan. Maybe I get it. Maybe I don't. Help me to understand," I pleaded.

At that stage of our discussions, the bell would invariably ring and we would be off to our respective classes. We always seemed to need more time so we could explain ourselves to each other.

Chapter 11:
"Ms. M."

*W*hen I became the department chair, I observed the teachers in my department as part of the responsibility of being the chair. As a result, I observed and evaluated Ms. M.'s class. I did so with trepidation. Megan personified original. I couldn't imagine telling Ms. M. what she should do to improve. She made up her own mind about everything and wanted her students to do the same.

Most of the teachers I knew and worked with were good in the classroom in their own way. As expected, Ms. M. was unique. Ms. M. had no compunction telling students what she thought. I was more reserved about giving my opinion in class. It was refreshing to hear a teacher tell students what she really believed, without playing the 'devil's advocate' game. She goaded her students into thinking for themselves.

In Ms. M.'s classroom, there were no lectures. She employed a variety of teaching strategies, sans lecturing. Megan abhorred depositing information into students' heads. She was an early apostle of critical thinking, deploring the methodology of feeding students with data that they did not have to think about. Megan compelled her students into thinking about all sources of knowledge including their teachers and especially what she, Ms. M., told them. She placed herself under her students' critical microscope.

I have finally come to believe that Megan is right when she says that teachers have biases and interpret events through personal lenses. In faculty meetings, Megan asked rhetorically, "We all make inferences and arrive at hypotheses, so why not share our educated guesses with each other and our students. What are we afraid of? There are biases in everything we say and do."

I tried to keep my views to myself when I first started teaching, but gradually shared with students some of what I thought. Right from the beginning, Megan did not hesitate and had no reservations about unabashedly telling people what she believed to be true.

In one of our discussions, Megan asserted to me, "As long as students can speak their piece without retribution for doing so, then no harm is done when teachers state their opinions. Indeed, Mark, it could stimulate students to think about what one believes to be so. We act on our assumptions of truth—our presumptions. The students might actually learn something if they test their teacher's thinking as well as their own."

She added, "As long as I don't grade my students on their opinions, especially if they have reasons and evidence for what they believe, then why not be honest with each other instead of contending that we are being unbiased. I am convinced that it is impossible to keep our interpretations out of the classroom. We all have biases Mark. Don't you have them? Of course, I believe you do and everyone else has them also. We cannot hide them, and I think we are just fooling ourselves when we think we can be completely objective. Sorry, Mark, but being neutral on important issues is impossible and to argue otherwise is absurd, so you might as well fess up."

Megan was able to use the "Tell them where you stand" approach to challenge her students' thinking. I never could quite pull it off though I tried gradually to have my students test their views against mine. However, when I provided my opinion to students it stopped the discussion. It was as if the "Guru" had spoken. By the end of my teaching career, I realized that it was virtually impossible for me to keep my views out of the classroom. Maybe others could. I could not. I have come to believe that teachers wear who they are and what they believe all over them. Megan knew this and over time I came to agree with her.

My half-way effort may have been a good way for me, because it was me. Megan, though, went all the way—which is what she seemed to do in everything she did. Megan helped some of our faculty recognize that we have biases and that even though we make a valiant effort to keep our views out of the classroom, the biases seep in nonetheless. Megan went even further, "A teacher's views are and should be part of the conversation. We are members of the class too."

I was not quite as bold as Megan or as sure of my views as she was. Before my thinking evolved more in her direction, I said, "Megan, I am not yet convinced that you are right about that. I believe we can establish fact and truth. We must be able to or why else are we teaching. So, I see your point but for the most part I disagree with what you are saying."

Megan often became frustrated with dissent, mine or anyone else's. "Damn it Mark, your biases are still in the classroom whether you admit it or not. Teachers cannot keep their views out of the classroom. Our preconceptions permeate much of what we do, so why not expose them so students can critically think for themselves. They can then make up their own minds about their teacher's views. Students are smarter than you think they are, Mr. M., they really are."

Continuing to make sure I got the point, Megan claimed that through her approach students could defend themselves against teachers who were propagating their beliefs in the classroom. Megan contended, "Teachers who say they are just giving the facts seldom are. If you watch them and listen to them long enough, you will see their enunciation of 'facts' emanates from their presumptions. Everyone has a camera through which they look at the world. A perspective if you will. So, we should all just be upfront about it."

There are all kinds of theories afloat in the education world as to how to teach. Some of the social studies teachers I have worked with deliver structured lectures and then handle questions after delivering information. Others give mini-lectures interspersed with discussion. Some teachers are highly experiential using the students' interests to lead to the subject matter. Still others ask questions requiring the students to come up with the answers. Then there are those who believe giving their own analyses and identifying opinion as such, while allowing and even encouraging students to state their hypotheses and tentative conclusions, provide a platform for critical thought and critical thinking to develop. Megan practiced the latter.

Megan used the "Tell them what you think and let the students debate" approach effectively. Students found it strange at first because teachers generally do not come right out and say, "This is my opinion." Megan did. Some teachers do not provide for student voices in the classroom. Megan encouraged them, indeed, triggered them. Ms. M.'s ideas so stimulated some of her students that they could not help but think.

This process disordered students who had pre-conceived beliefs—while it liberated those open to changing their views when evidence warranted.

The students also soon learned not to make sexist comments in Megan's classroom. Ms. M. made it abundantly clear that comments about gender needed to be defended with a rationale. She would ask, "Do you have support for that statement? And, if you do, does one premise lead to the next?"

If the students did not have evidence to support what they said, they would meekly evoke a "Nope." Megan usually followed with an encouraging, "Try stating your argument again."

Some of what Ms. M. perceived as sexist jolted her students. Megan challenged anything she labeled as sexism. She demonstrated to faculty and students alike how words like "baby," "honey," or even "dear" could be derogatory. And, that "whore" had no male counter-part.

Megan objected to students "ogling" each other. Teens with active libidos found this difficult to control, but they found out that in Ms. M.'s classroom such behavior was out of the class's boundary and invited the teacher's reproach.

Students sometimes try to prod a teacher in order to incite a teacher's metaphorical goat. Ms. M.'s students knew that anything that smacked of sexism got to Megan's innards. Her students knew better than to go there. From the first day of class, students learned what Ms. M.'s limits were and not to exceed them. There was no "getting the teacher angry" in Ms. M.'s classroom. If the students tried, they found out what "or else" and anger meant.

Megan's pent up energy could burst. It didn't happen often, but it was known to happen when students crossed, pressed against, or even brushed against their teacher's "don't go there" line. Year after year, students told her future students to "Beware of testing Ms. M.'s patience." Few tried.

Some students did not like experiencing the cognitive dissonance in Ms. M.'s classes. Other students flourished in her classroom reaching new heights of independent thought. Several parents objected to their children learning to think on their own. Yet, thinking for themselves was precisely the kind of thought Megan was trying to encourage among her students. After being in Megan's classroom for a while, parents discerned growth in their children's thinking which blunted their criticism of this "renegade" teacher.

Megan taught in Bailey T. S. Memorial High School for 30 years, from 1970 to 2000, long enough to be vested in a pension. Like Derek, Megan had plenty to work with in her social studies classes during the momentous early 1970's. In the fall of 1970, teachers and students still talked about the tragic events that took place at Kent State University in Ohio where four protestors against the war in Vietnam were killed and others wounded.

A picture of a female teenager kneeling over one of those who had been shot added relevancy for Ms. M.'s students. The poignant photo circulated world-wide. Megan expressed horror in her class. Her students gasped as they grasped the point.

The discussions in Megan's classroom were vigorous and sharp. Some of the students wanted to get active outside of class. They debated whether to organize protests in response to American planes crossing borders and bombing in Cambodia. The students became alarmed in the early 1970's with the prospect of the conflicts in Southeast Asia expanding into Laos, Cambodia, and possibly elsewhere.

Megan's students examined the vocabulary they used to describe events. "Was it a war in Vietnam or a conflict?" "Had Congress declared war?" "Did Congress need to if it was called a conflict or something other than a war?" "Does calling it a war rather than a conflict make it more serious or just sound more serious?" Megan spread these and other questions throughout her classes prompting student thinking. At Ms. M.'s urging, her students examined everything that the prevailing political culture's boundaries would allow. At times, her classes stretched and exceeded Gorham's outer limits.

Students rallied others through calls for "solidarity," a common contemporary catchword. Ms. M. knew how to help her students relate to and learn from events they were witnessing and then turn their knowledge into positive actions.

Some of her students' actions could have gotten Megan into trouble. However, she was so effective in teaching that the students expressed to their parents that they were learning important concepts and lessons. Her effectiveness in teaching staved off the censors. In addition, it was the early 1970's when critical thought in the classroom was encouraged. The controversies of the Vietnam era spilled into high school classrooms beckoning debate. Megan's classroom spurred both agreement and dissent. Ms. M.'s students reveled in the discourse.

Megan's students even thought critically about the school's nickname—the Revolutionaries, or the shortened, "The Revs." Their critique bordered Bailey High's divide for tolerance. In an editorial in the school newspaper, *Bailey's Black, Red, and White Gazette*, the editors wrote, "How can our nickname be 'Revolutionaries' when both Gorham and its high school, Bailey High, conduct their reactionary business as if in the eighteenth century—no, sorry—in the seventeenth century when witches were burned." Through the years, the school administration barely tolerated the Bailey High newspaper emblazoned in black, red, and white, the school colors. In the years Megan Straffa taught in the high school, most of the editors had her as a teacher. Neither the community nor the school's administration were able to make the connection.

The events during the summer of 1973 added kindle to the hotbed of discourse that Ms. M.'s classroom hosted. The American public learned increasingly about the break-ins at the Watergate Hotel in Washington, D.C. These events eventually led to President Richard Nixon's resignation in August of 1974. Nixon became the first president to resign from the nation's highest executive office.

Nixon's appointed vice president, Gerald Ford, replaced Nixon upon the latter's resignation. Ford subsequently pardoned his predecessor prompting protests. Ford had his own problems as president but nothing like Nixon.

Later in the decade, Jimmy Carter ascended to the presidency. President Carter attempted to confront a perceived "energy crisis." He started wearing sweaters in the White House to signal that the United States and the world were approaching scarcity in clean natural resources. Critics claimed there was no crisis. The crisis-deniers took their sweaters off and turned up the heat on both Carter and in their offices and homes.

In 1979, Carter met a crisis of his own when some Iranians took Americans stationed in Tehran, Iran, hostage for 444 days. The various media's fixation on captive Americans further damaged the president's popularity.

The Iranian "hostage crisis," with media's relentless coverage, contributed to the election of Ronald Reagan to the presidency in 1980. Megan's response was "How can Americans elect that guy. A Hollywood actor—second-rate at that. I don't get it. Or maybe I do get it which frightens me even more."

In addition to discussing important events of the 1970's and 1980's in class, Megan personally found both Presidents Ronald Reagan and George H. W. Bush to be against those things she believed were important for the progress of women. Megan expressed her disapproval of the Reagan and Bush presidencies in the classroom as well as out. Her vocal opinions and advocacies upset some politically potent people in the Gorham community. Megan, reluctant to give in to political pressure, "doubled down" and upped the debate temperature in her classroom. As chair of the department, I tried to provide cover for Megan with parents and members of the community who complained about what was transpiring in Ms. M.'s classroom. Megan sloughed off the complaints. She kept doing in her classroom what she perceived as her job.

President William J. Clinton's administration did nothing to improve Megan's notion of establishment politics, or escape her cynical critique. Although Megan agreed with some of what Clinton did from 1993 through the rest of the decade, she found his behavior with women repulsive. Her disparaging view of politicians penetrated her classroom.

On the day Megan Straffa left Bailey High in June of 2000 she gazed into room 223, her usual classroom, scanned the desks one last time and left the school building. I have always wondered what she was searching for as she glanced through the door window. On her way to the parking lot, she said, "I have 30 years in. It is time for me to do something else. I can't stand the two-faced political corruption any more. Both political parties are corrupt. They just represent the interests of the lobbyists and the plutocrats. I have to do something else to bring about change."

Megan's distaste and disillusionment for what politics had become had worn on her. She had also tired of the critics who tried to pressure her into becoming someone she was not. Ms. M. left teaching in the year in which a minority of voters would elect George W. Bush president of the United States.

At the end of June of the year 2000, Megan searched for a new place for her to be. She did not tell me where she was going or what she would be doing. Yet, Megan did make the "why" she was leaving teaching unmistakable. "I have to work, using all my energy, to advance women's rights nationally and throughout the world." Her sincerity bled through her words.

Megan retired convinced that she could not do what she

believed she needed to do teaching school. She told me, "I have to do something else. I have to become active to make a difference in this world."

I learned later that Megan had become an advocate for equal rights for women, specifically trying to get the Equal Rights Amendment ratified in the United States of America while simultaneously working for women's educational opportunities throughout the globe.

After Megan Straffa left Bailey T. S. Memorial High School on a rainy day in June, 2000, I did not see Megan or hear from her again for a long time.

Chapter 12:
Ken

*I*t seemed as if Ken Lewiston had been teaching in Bailey High forever. He had been there for ten years when I arrived in 1970. The students loved Mr. K. They absolutely loved him like no other teacher I ever observed past or present.

Along with the students' admiration for Ken, I envied his teaching methods. They were different from anything I had seen as a teacher or experienced as a student. If Megan was single-minded in her teaching methodology, Ken, on the other hand, employed whatever method in his multi-method box that was necessary to get students thinking. I could not do what Ken did and have never seen another teacher who was as effective with high school students.

It was strange at first sitting in on his classes. New students grasped Ken's intense sincerity right from the start, so any strangeness soon evaporated. It took adults longer to catch on to Ken's style. Some never did.

Ken started teaching soon after attending a state college where teacher education was an emphasis. If there is such a phenomenon as an instinctive teacher, Ken exemplified it. He was informed in a variety of subjects, passionate about what he taught, creative in his various teaching methods, and invariably sensitive to his students. Ken cared deeply about

.udent, and the world in which he taught. If Ken had a
.lt, it was that he was "too" sensitive. Ken brooded when a
class did not go well—he did not want to miss a single chance
to help young people grow into knowledgeable, active citizens.

When I first met Ken, he must have been in his early 30's.
He was already balding but did not seem the least bit self-
conscious about it. He rode a bicycle to school which kept him
in good shape. His thin, gangly frame fit tightly in his well-
conditioned five feet eleven inches.

Even though he most likely lived close to Bailey High in
order to bike to work, I never knew where he lived. He wore
dark rimmed glasses as I did which gave us both that studious
look.

Ken's teaching methods were innovative, even for the
experimental 1960's and early 1970's. He arranged his
classroom desks in a circle. He peppered students with
questions sprinkled with spicy, descriptive language. The
students stretched and expanded their vocabulary in Ken's
class. And because it was Mr. K., and his students learned
something new each day, even parents who only wanted the
schools to "teach my children the subject matter—nothing else"
did not complain about what Ken did in the classroom.

Ken engaged, challenged, interested and enticed his
students into new ways of thinking. He encouraged them to be
active and informed.

In my third year teaching at the school, I sat in on one of
Ken's classes in early September of 1973. During the
Watergate hearings that summer, President Richard Nixon
looked like he was in big trouble after the revelation of tape
recordings in the Oval office and the "smoking gun" tape
indicating that there may have been criminality on the part of
some in Nixon's administration.

I wanted to see how Ken was going to handle the

controversial issues endemic to the Watergate hearings. In Ken's classes, there were no "observers," so when I visited his class he involved me in the discussion. I tried to be careful and keep my interpretations to myself, but sitting in Ken's circled desks facing each participant it was impossible to hide intellectually or otherwise. If Derek was effective at getting students to think outside the lines, Ken was even better at broadening, stirring, and swelling the elasticity of thought.

In his classes, Ken helped his students by gently nudging them out of closed intellectual boxes. He would then skillfully slide the students into the new boxes they had created for themselves. He then coaxed his students to create new hypotheses so they would have to think their way out of their newly created intellectual straight-jackets. Ken exemplified teaching genius at work.

Ken had mastered the art of generating cognitive dissonance in his students so they would have to arrive at their own conclusions. As he surveyed his students' thinking, they revealed their thoughts allowing him to challenge them to think further and for themselves. There was no other way out of his classroom. Both Ken and Megan developed the teaching of independent thinking, albeit each performing in their own art.

Through Ken's brilliant teaching, the conceptual problems grew in complexity. The students' thinking flourished. Ken's classroom channeled intellectual wizardry—thinking that progressed and progressed—revealing previously hidden ideas that the students did not know they had. Students yielded "ahas" as they pulled new concepts and hypotheses out of previously unknown or hidden places in their mental recesses. I found concepts in my thinking in Ken's classes that I, too, did not know were there. Ken sent all in his classroom searching for thoughts long closed in their cranial crevices—thoughts

77

that emerged through his searching questions. Ken modeled the scholar as teacher.

During the Watergate congressional hearings, I arrived in the classroom just as the students chose their places in the circle. Ken no longer had to tell them to "circle up" because in his classroom the students did not have to be told after the first day of class that they were expected to participate. And, participate they did.

In September 1973, Ken could smell the impeachment of a president and he wanted the students to understand what may occur as a result of the Watergate hearings. He started with a question: "What is impeachment?"

A student reached for an answer, "Mr. K., isn't it when the president is taken out of office depending on how Congress votes?" As Ken's students got into an issue buzzing infused the classroom.

Ken invariably built on student responses whether right or wrong, never embarrassing any student for an incomplete or incorrect answer. So, he then asked the class, "Does anyone have something to add to Janice's answer?"

Another student added. "The House of Representatives can vote to impeach a president, but the trial is held in the Senate where the senators decide on guilt and if the president should be removed for 'high crimes'."

"Have any presidents ever been impeached?"

"Yes," said another student. "President Andrew Johnson was impeached in 1868, but he was not convicted."

"He was acquitted by one vote," said another student.

"Have any other presidents been impeached?" Ken asked.

"Not yet!" As a student chorus rung out with smiling faces, anticipating that it might happen in their lifetime.

Ken inserted questions to make sure students were paying attention, "Have any women presidents been impeached?"

Laughter followed, as students hummed in unison, "No, because there haven't been any women presidents. Come on Mr. K. you can't trick us."

With a soft smile, Ken emitted his classic, "Hmmmmm," which the students loved because they knew that Mr. K. was conveying approval in his own inimitable way. The students had not been fooled nor had Mr. K. fooled them. Instead, he had enlightened his students engaging them in new ways of thinking.

Ken never hushed his students, letting them emote when they scored. They hadn't and didn't fall for his feint. A slow respectful hiss followed their victory over ignorance. Ken's covert delight morphed into a surreptitious grin which his students waited for because it meant that they got it.

In the class that day, there were a lot of incorrect or incomplete answers, but Ken did not treat them as wrong. Instead, he constructed a foundation with each response. His students tasted their incremental learning.

In Ken's classes, students were not afraid to respond, ineluctably generating and testing hypotheses. Ken was kind and sensitive to each student in his class treating any attempted response with respect. He related to each student as the individuals they were, savoring their individuality. The terminology "we are family" is heard often—in Ken's class it rendered real.

Ken did make sure the students knew the facts. He summarized with them: "The House of Representatives impeaches; the Senate tries the case. The Chief Justice of the Supreme Court of the United States serves as the judge. It takes two-thirds of the Senate to convict. No president of the United States has ever been convicted of 'high crimes and misdemeanors.'"

Then he would follow with a series of questions: "What are

high crimes and misdemeanors? How are they proved? Why has no president who has been impeached been convicted?"

Within the 48-minute period, Ken moved beyond factual matters to the larger issues embodied in the separation of powers, checks and balances, and other concepts immersed in *The Constitution of the United States.*

In his classes, Ken queried his students on right and wrong, "What is the moral thing to do? What is immoral? Who decides? What does ethical mean? What is unethical behavior? What is the difference between moral and ethical behavior? If you have to choose, is it more important to live ethically or morally?" Watching Ken work, you could hear the students' mental and emotional wheels turning. Ken's reflectors were turning too as he created a community of learners.

Ken enabled his students to work out their contradictions by illustrating that they had them. In his classes, Ken characteristically challenged his students to think further by saying, "If you believe what you just said, then how can you believe the opposite that you said in a previous statement?"

With a kind smile, understanding that resolving inconsistencies can be puzzling to learners new to such problem solving, Ken challenged the student to think further, "That is classic Orwellian 'double think'. How can you believe both to be true?" The student would have to clarify the logic, sometimes with the help of other students. Mr. K. let them figure it out for themselves—in life they would have to. Ken painted intellectual pageantry framed so students remembered the learning experience and how to get from A to B to C.

For high school students, being in Ken's class was to be immersed deeply into the complexity of the subject matter. Ken was able to pull it off. He was not only popular with the students—he was good.

I learned a lot from Ken. He challenged my thinking in his

class and out as he did his students. He was always on as a teacher in the classroom, in the lunchroom, in the corridor, and in informal settings.

I wondered how always being "on" wore on Ken. I had a family to take me away now and then. Ken did not seem to have something outside of school, but I really didn't know. I didn't ask and Ken didn't say.

I became chair of the department in the fall of 1973, in part, because Ken did not want the job. The rest of us in the department wanted him, but he did not want the paperwork or the power that came with the position. He also said he did not need the extra money to support his small apartment, his bike and himself. Besides, he was happy in the classroom where he could spend each precious moment with his students.

Chapter 13:
"Mr. K."

*K*en Lewiston taught in Bailey Memorial from the fall of 1960 to February 1985. In his classes, he asked the what, where, when, who and how questions, and as with Derek Randallston, Mr. K. investigated mostly the why. "Why did this happen? Why is it important?" He showered questions throughout the students in his classes. Questions that appeared general were sometimes aimed at a particular student's interests. Ken's students learned to relish the questioning, and learn from Mr. K.'s teaching. He coached his students to think further than they thought possible. His students frequently exceeded Mr. K.'s already high expectations as they generated innovative hypotheses. When this happened, Ken beamed.

In Mr. K.'s classes, the students talked most of the time—the teacher less. The students were invariably involved, interested, and joyfully participating in class and in their community. Ken spoke when necessary pumping more questions or providing information so the students would think critically and probe deeper.

Some of his students carried the methodologies Ken used into other classes. As with Megan Straffa's students, Ken's students also took new ideas and questions home to dinner table discussions where their parents solicited where the students got the ideas and skill in asking stimulating and sometimes provocative questions. Some of the parents embraced the experience their sons and daughters had in Ken's classes. Disengaged parents never inquired.

Ken helped the students realize that they needed to check things out, not believe everything they hear, find and compare multiple sources, and check their assumptions at the classroom door. He encouraged students to "Find one, two, three sources; verify them, and then check again. Think, think, and think some more."

When the Vietnam War controversy attained its apex in the 1960's and 1970's, Ken nudged his students to see both sides. "Why did we go into Vietnam?" "Was it for economic reasons?" "Was it to contain Communism?" And, his favorite questions for students, "What do you think?" And, "Why do you think that?"

Upon the United States leaving Vietnam in 1975, Ken asked his students to analyze whether the conflict and loss of life was worth the sacrifice. Then, after the ground breaking for the Vietnam Veterans Memorial in 1982, the names of 58,191 Americans who lost their lives in Vietnam were engraved sacredly into that hallowed wall. Ken asked the question again to groups of students who were children when the conflict ended seven years prior— "Was the Vietnam conflict worth it?" Some students said it was, others said it was not. Ken listened and encouraged all sides to offer their opinions and evidence.

Ken recommended that his students, traveling to Washington D. C. with their parents or in a group, go to the Memorial and reflect on what it is like to see all those names.

"They are people just like us," Ken said. "Just people like us who went to war but they did not return home alive. Think about that. We need to humanize those names on the wall. They were someone's child, some were parents, and all were a member of a family." And, then when he said, "They were someone's students," his voice uncharacteristically broke. Ken didn't lecture very often, but on this subject he did and did so eloquently.

Shortly after the Vietnam Veterans Memorial opened to visitors, Ken traveled to the wall in Washington, D. C. to honor those who died in Southeast Asia fighting Communism. He told me how travelers to the wall responded to seeing a name they recognized. With a voice barely audible, Ken said as his voice shook, "Many of those honoring the wall and the names on it caressed the imprint of a person they loved." Ken did not shed tears without reason, but when he spoke the word "love" heartbroken water streamed down his cheeks.

In Ken's classes, the students contested each other on virtually every subject. Likewise, Ken as readily challenged his colleagues to thrash through issues with each other. However, in the beginning of February of 1985, Ken told me in a voice that left no room for debate or further deliberation, "I need some time off to take care of something."

I asked Ken, "Will we need a long-term substitute or just someone for a couple of days?"

Ken responded in a subdued, barely audible voice, "Mark, I recommend the substitute be employed for an indefinite period."

Ken seldom used sick days, so I knew something unusual had happened or was about to happen.

Teaching was the essence of Ken's life. He would only vacate his classroom if he believed he absolutely had to. For some reason Ken needed to leave soon and do so without a return date.

As Ken took leave, he took some things with him, mostly memorabilia, letters, and pictures that students had given him during his years of teaching. After he left, some tearful students asked about him. It was painfully clear that they missed their teacher. I and other staff told them that we knew nothing, which at the time was the truth.

After a couple of weeks of not hearing anything, which seemed an eternity, we became concerned. We wanted him back in school because we felt barren without him.

Both the faculty and the students missed Ken's spark in the classroom. His colleagues valued his insightful and trenchant comments in our meetings. Ken had the ability to get us all to think deeply about our work with students and the content we were teaching.

After what I thought was enough time anguishing about how to contact Ken, I decided to call him. I tried several times without reaching him, and there was no way to leave a message. The school did have his mailing address for summer checks and essential paperwork, so I tried that.

About a month after I wrote to Ken and heard nothing, I received a phone call at home from a friend of Ken's who told me that "Ken had died of pneumonia which resulted from the Acquired Immune Deficiency Syndrome (AIDS) virus." I was shocked, in denial, and subdued by the news.

When I recovered enough to ask, his friend said, "A service will be held next Saturday in a community center about ten miles away. Mr. Blenchard, I am sad to tell you that once some people knew how he died they refused to host the service.

"Also, Mr. Blenchard, Ken told me before he died that he would like to have you speak at his funeral service. Would you please tell the rest of the faculty about Ken's passing and come to speak about Ken and his teaching at Bailey High? Ken loved teaching in Bailey High with the students and with you and the rest of the faculty.

"Mr. Blenchard, the service will be private. You and a small group of friends are the only people invited. You would be the only one representing the school."

I chose not to tell the faculty or the students about Ken's death and how he died. I was ashamed of myself for being unwilling to do so. I trembled as I thought about what might happen if people knew—gutless I know, but I was terrified at the prospect of the public "Scarlet Letter."

At the time, in the middle of the 1980's, we were just beginning to learn about the disease that led to Ken's death. We knew enough in 1985, though, to know that the news about AIDS was not good. People who did not understand the illness often shunned those who had it and those who were in any identifiable way associated with the sickness. Some members of the public called for quarantining those with the disease.

Thus, I opted for craven silence in not telling anyone in Bailey High. I cowered in the face of what I thought might happen. I asked myself, "Should I even go to speak at his funeral?"

After the phone call, I went downstairs to speak with Ana. "Ana, I have some bad news. I just learned that Ken Lewiston has died."

"Oh my God, Mark, how?"

"A friend of his informed me that he died from AIDS."

"Is that the new disease mostly men get? I don't know much about it. What is it and how do you get it?"

"I don't know much about it either, or the answers to those questions. But that is what Ken's friend reported that Ken died from."

"Mark is there anything we can or should do?"

"I have been asked by his friend to speak at Ken's service."

"Did you say yes? You said yes, of course."

"No. I did not give a yes or no. I don't think I am going to do it though."

"You should do it," Ana said without hesitating." Mark, you

told me that Ken never talked about his family. It was like he didn't have one. You, other faculty, and his students have been his family. You, at least, should be there to represent yourself and the rest of the school. Do this for yourself, if not for Ken. I don't want to see you live with this forever. Please do it, Mark, please."

"But Ana, what if the school board hears about it and doesn't like it. I could get fired or just let go? Mitchell hasn't retired yet, and I must be on his list somewhere. He is the kind of macho guy who really wouldn't approve of my going to a service like this one much less speaking."

"Ken was a good guy, a friend of yours, and a wonderful teacher. You owe it to him and to yourself. I know I am repeating myself, but you have to do it."

"I can't, Ana, I can't. Joel is 14 now, loves his school and teachers, and does not want to move to another school. Neither do I. And, Suzie, well, she just started junior high and any move for her would be unsettling with her anxiety and all. I just cannot do it and be fair to my family and myself. I love my job. I couldn't live if I couldn't teach."

"Do what you have to do, Mark, but I think you ought to speak for Ken. We will figure something out as a family if something happens with your job. You can always teach in another town. Besides, I have my job teaching kindergarten. I could find another job if I need to. Or, I could set up a child care or pre-school business."

"I don't want you to have to do that—get laid off, quit your job, or have to set up a business."

"I could and I would, Mark."

"They might get you too and ruin your reputation because you are connected to me. You would be tainted and guilty by association. If they let me go, you are the next logical step. Besides, if they want to save some money they would get rid of you. Hasn't the school board said they only needed two kindergarten teachers rather than three? They could rotate two kindergarten teachers and cover all the kindergarteners. People are having fewer children so enrollment is decreasing. We could both be out of a job if I did it. I can't risk it. We can't risk it."

I worried the night away, tossing and turning, wishing for some sunlight so I could get up and do something else rather than worry about whether I was doing the right thing or not.

The service was scheduled for the coming Saturday. I had told Ken's friend that I would call him at the beginning of the week and let him know if I would speak at the service. He probably expected me to attend even if I did not speak. I had tried to sleep on it to no avail. After thinking about the options, I decided that I would not speak and I would not attend. I was afraid of being seen. I knew I was melting under invisible pressure but I thought I had to for my job and my family's welfare. The service would and could go on without me.

I did not call Ken's friend. I was mortified at the prospect of saying "No" to a human voice—a real live friend of Ken's. Instead, I wrote a brief letter to the address I had been given. I later regretted sending the letter, and not calling. I didn't even have the courage to tell him over the phone that I wouldn't be attending. Instead, I wrote:

"I will not be attending the service on Saturday. You have my condolences for your loss. I, the faculty at Bailey T. S. Memorial High School, and the students will miss Ken.

Sincerely, Mark Blenchard."

I had chickened out, and I chose the least personal way of doing so. I just couldn't face even a phone call with Ken's friend. I determined that I could not publicly bereave Ken—a teacher I had worked with, learned from, and respected all those years. I slithered away from my responsibility as a friend and a teacher.

The Monday after Ken's observance nearly undid me. I walked into my first period class, and saw a class full of somber faces. Almost in unison, they asked, "Why didn't you tell us about Mr. K.? We found out what happened. Billy Brown's brother does clean up at the community center where the service was held. We heard you weren't there but were invited. Mr. Blenchard, even though we weren't invited, we students would have gone to pay tribute to Mr. K. We would have spoken for him. If they wouldn't let us in, we would have stood around outside with our heads bowed. Instead of you or us being there, nobody from the school was there to speak for Mr. K. Mr. M., you weren't there for Mr. K. He was a friend of yours and a great teacher. And, he died without us even knowing or being there for him after he lived for us. Mr. M., you knew about it, did not tell us, did not speak over him, and did not go to the service. We are so sad about Mr. K. And, we are so disappointed in you." This was by far my worse day teaching—ever—and it didn't get any better for the rest of the week or for some time after.

As tears flowed that day in my classes, I had no response for being a coward and not being there for my friend and colleague. I had succumbed to what I thought might happen to me. I had let fear prevent me from doing what I knew was the right thing to do. I did not want to suck up to conformity, but I had. My students knew that I had withered because of my fear of social repute and losing my job. I knew it too. In each class that week, I was met with the rustle of grief and searing disbelief that "their" teacher did not attend his friend's funeral and did not speak for him because of fear. The students surely would have celebrated Ken's life, and been willing to accept the consequences. I shook and shrunk at the prospect of doing what I should have done. The students had no fear when the right thing was in front of them to do.

I had just enough in me to go to school each day that week. I thought it would take a while for me to get over my cowardness. When you forsake yourself, as I had, confidence in who you are and what you stand for bleeds dry. I have never gotten over betraying my friend and myself by not attending and speaking at Ken's service. The students' disappointed murmuring that day has never left me. I do not want to ever experience and feel like that again.

Ken was a teacher of teachers. I learned so much from him. My lack of courage in speaking for him haunts me, and will continue to do so until I find the backbone to do what Ken would do.

Ken Lewiston died at age 46. I hoped that I could one day have the gumption to do what I knew to be the right thing to do without regard for the consequences. I had something to live up to. I wanted another chance.

Chapter 14:
Cheryl

heryl Wattsen, an English teacher in Bailey T. S. Memorial High School, was by most accounts a good one. Some students and parents thought she was too demanding. In her mind, however, Cheryl wanted her students to write well and read critically which made her classes challenging for some students. Domineering parents objected to the deflated grades that their "can do no wrong" children sometimes received.

Cheryl joined the school's faculty in the fall of 1973, the year I became chair of the social studies department. She was almost a decade older than the rest of us on the Bailey faculty at the time. Before teaching, Cheryl tried retail sales, real estate brokering, and selling insurance. She succeeded in everything she tried, so she decided to try selling ideas to high school students. As she discovered, teaching high school students was a much more difficult task than moving products around.

Tall and erect, Cheryl's bearing announced a stately appearance. For some students, just watching her walk in the classroom intimidated them. Her palpable attractiveness added to her stature making her look formidable and untouchable, especially to teenagers.

Cheryl's father, a retired army officer, had served in Korea.

He was later stationed in Germany where her mother taught English on an army base. Cheryl's family moved around a lot as military families are wont to do. She added relevance to her English classes with stories of exotic places she had been. Her students dreamed about traveling in her footsteps, and learning what she had. For students and faculty alike, Ms. C. manifested the educated person.

Private and reserved, Cheryl mostly kept her personal views and feelings to herself. She, like Megan, was not an easy person to know but seemingly for disparate reasons. When asked about her stony, apparently impenetrable visage, she said, "Anyone really interested in who I am should study the books I read and the literature I assign in class. The books I select will tell you a lot about who I am. So, if you really do want to know me, then read the books I do and have. Or, if you want to peruse the books in my carrel, then that might help but not as much as reading them. I am a reader. I read all of the time. I read in a variety of genres. That's who I am. That fact and the volumes I devour should tell you all you need to know about me." Cheryl was a lot about what "you needed to know," and that you didn't need to know much more about her than she willingly disclosed and displayed.

Cheryl did not crack jokes in class, although when she was with other faculty members she reveled in a mischievous and salty sense of humor. Yet, even when she filled a room with her humor, Cheryl revealed little about herself.

Cheryl had chortling down pat. She could chortle with the best of them to the delight of all within hearing distance. Cheryl was so good at it that the teacher's room's walls crackled with her colleagues' appreciative roar. Her fellow teachers liked and valued her as a friend and teacher.

In one discussion with me, Cheryl reported, "I was a good student in high school, and I expect my students to be the same.

I realize that I am a stickler for rules and details, all kinds of rules, grammatical or otherwise. As a child in a military family, I know all about discipline and obedience and want to teach my students the same traits that have helped me."

Cheryl explained further, "Following the rules in high school helped me to succeed as a student and to be called a 'good student' whether I really learned very much or not. I realized in college that in order to write well, I needed to break some of the rules. However, in order to break the rules, I have to know what they are. So, I teach my students the rules and then I teach them which ones they can break. Writing well often requires rule breaking."

As a student, Cheryl knew which rules she could break. This pragmatic knowledge carried over into employment in a school system. She quickly identified the school rules she could break and which ones should not be broken. This is how she survived in the highly politicized Gorham school system.

Cheryl attended a state research university where she studied English literature. She then earned a Master's degree in Humanities. After she finished her studies, she tried selling clothes, land and security. Even though she was good at selling things, Cheryl found business unfulfilling. Her life was built around reading and writing, so she thought she might enjoy teaching. When I first met her in 1973, she was in her first year teaching.

Cheryl married prior to joining the Bailey High faculty. Her husband, Cliff, a lawyer, accompanied her to some school events. In social meetings, Cliff did not have much to say but his quiet mien did not mean he wasn't following the discussion. When he did talk, everyone listened.

Even though Ms. C. seemed remote to students, when they were in trouble they felt they could go to her. For some reason, maybe because she was an attractive female with an open mind about seemingly everything, potentially sexually active students would stop in to see her and frequently ask for advice. She appeared to be worldly, approachable, and inviting. This appealed to some students, especially those who needed someone to listen to them, and maybe even to advise them on what to do.

Cheryl watched carefully what she advised students to do. She usually consulted with Cliff before offering specific advice, especially if it might raise questions of legality.

One specific case early in her second year at Bailey High, though, threatened to finish her career at our school. She generally followed the rules, but in this case the rules weren't clear. After this incident, she exercised more caution.

In a private discussion with me, she said, "Mark, here is what happened. A female student, who will remain unnamed, came to me seeking information about birth control."

In the 1970's, birth control advice for teens could be difficult to come by and could give any adult who provided birth control or even information about it some problems. However, this time when asked by a seemingly sophisticated and mature student, Cheryl told me, "Without checking with Cliff, I offered some guidance on how to protect against pregnancy and disease. It seemed to me to be a reasonable and responsible thing to do. I should have realized that I was breaking an unwritten rule in my rule-centered life that could not easily be mended.

"After consulting with me, the teen and her boyfriend went to the local drug store, obtained over the counter birth control, went to the girl's house because no one was home, and had intercourse on the living room rug. The couple carefully covered the rug with towels hoping to leave no trace of what occurred. Unexpectedly, the student's mother came home and found the two teens deeply into the act."

Cheryl continued, "The girl reported to me that when the student's mother walked in on them she said, 'What the hell are you doing?' The paramours were as surprised as the mother was."

At this point, I could not help but have a smile on my face. Cheryl did not see the humor and said, "Mark, this is not funny."

I responded guiltily, "Sorry."

Cheryl proceeded to explain what happened next, "The mother screamed at the young man, 'Get out of here' as he tried to find his clothes.

"Should I continue Mark?"

"Yes."

"After the mother kicked the boyfriend out, the student's mother asked her daughter if the two were using birth control. 'Yes, mom, we were.' The student answered as if that condoned the act."

Cheryl paused for a moment, "Go on. Cheryl, please." I said.

"Her mother followed with the next logical question, 'Where did you get the birth control, and how did you know about it?'

"Apparently, Mark, after some intense motherly questioning, the student responded, 'Ms. C. told me where I could find birth control.' Her daughter later told me that the look on her mother's face made it clear that she was not happy with the answer that a teacher was the source of this kind of information.

"The student responded to her mother, 'Ma, Ms. C. was just trying to be helpful so I would not get pregnant or get a disease.' And, that was what I was trying to do. Keep her from being hurt. Maybe I should not have done that, but at the time I thought that giving her the information on how to protect herself would help and was the right thing to do.

"The teen's mother was not assuaged. She picked up the

phone. The teen's mother called the school, talked to the principal, who then contacted me."

"What happened next, Cheryl? This does not sound good if the principal wanted to see you about giving out birth control information."

"Mark, you said, 'this does not sound good.' Well, that is an understatement. If the principal wanted to see me about what I told the student, I could be fired or worse. I did wonder what it could be about that he wanted to see me, because at that moment I was unaware of the parent contacting the principal. So, I called Cliff in case the principal had something in mind more than 'How has your day been, Cheryl?'

"I called Cliff. I reached him in his office and told him, 'The principal wants to see me immediately.'"

"Cliff responded, 'Do you know what it is about?'

"I told Cliff that 'I did not know, but I did talk to a student about birth control. That may be it, but I don't know.' That was enough to raise Cliff's legal antenna.

"Cliff advised me, 'Cheryl, if that is it, say very little—admit nothing—then find a way to get out of the office. We will talk further when I get home.' It was clear from his voice that I better find a way out of the principal's office and do so with dispatch if the issue is what I told the student about birth control and protecting herself."

"Ah, Cheryl, tell me the outcome of the meeting. I know you are an English teacher. You have sure built the suspense in this story. I need to know how it got resolved—assuming it did."

"Okay, Mark, I will. Here is, as we say in English classes, the denouement. You are smiling again."

"Sorry." I said as a grin remained on my face. I smiled because I was beginning to realize that Cheryl would not have been telling me this story if it had worked out badly. "I am a little slow now and then figuring things out. I need more details, Cheryl."

"Yes, indeed, my friend, you are often totally innocent in the ways of the world."

Cheryl continued the story. "After the principal and I exchanged greetings, I was confronted with what I said to the student. My worst fears were realized. I took Cliff's advice and all of a sudden was not feeling well. I told the principal, 'I am sorry. I am really not feeling well. I will get back to you as soon as I feel better, but I have to go now. I feel sick to my stomach. Sorry.' I got up and briskly walked out as in a hurry, which I was.

"Okay, Mark, here is the final chapter of this tale of woe narrowly avoided. Fortunately for all concerned, the girl in question did not get pregnant or contract disease. Her mother decided to drop the issue and not push it further—thank goodness! The principal did not want to pursue the issue either. He realized that I would fight for my job and would have legal assistance in doing so. The fact that the mother did not register a formal complaint allowed the principal and me to escape a no-win situation."

Cheryl learned from this encounter. After the close call, Cheryl stayed away from providing specific advice to students relating to anything sexual. Although students kept going to her for help with personal problems, Cheryl recognized when an issue could become problematic. Depending on the problem, Ms. C. sent students to certified professionals for assistance.

Cheryl continued to teach and teach well at Bailey High until she confronted a problem of her own. One that Cliff's legal skill was of little use in solving. When Cheryl started teaching she was in her early thirties. She looked younger than her chronological age. In Bailey High, Cheryl behaved more maturely than some faculty who were years older.

Cheryl comported herself as if she did not have many

problems with which to cope. So, when Cliff called me and Ana on a Sunday evening about Cheryl it was a surprise, because hardly anyone called on a Sunday evening before school the next day. Cheryl seemingly had it all together. She was the last person I expected to receive a panic-filled call about as the weekend was ending.

In a brief telephone call, Cliff said, "Mark, Cheryl is freaking out. I need you to come over if you can. Please bring Ana, too, if she can leave the children with someone."

Cliff would never ask us to leave our children unless he was really concerned with something. "Ana can't come but I can. We have no one to leave the children with. What is happening Cliff?"

"I will tell you when you get here. I cannot tell you right now."

"Cliff, I will be right there." I said as I hung up.

Racing out of my house, I told Ana what I knew, "Ana, Cliff has asked me to come over to his house. It is something about Cheryl. I don't know any more than that. I will be back as soon as I can."

I arrived at the Wattsen's house as quickly as I could. Cliff was waiting at the door. "What's up Cliff? It sounded over the phone like there is a problem with Cheryl. Is she sick or something?"

"Mark, please come in." Cliff said.

I took a seat on the couch. Cliff hesitated for a moment, but then began to explain, "I need to tell you something, but you have to keep it to yourself. It would kill Cheryl if it got out. And, Mark, because Ana couldn't come tonight, please don't even tell Ana what I am going to tell you. So, Mark, please don't tell anyone. I believe that the fewer people who know the better. Cheryl would be so embarrassed if others knew. And, tell me Mark, that this does not happen to people like us.

Please."

"I don't know about that Cliff, but whatever you tell me will be safe with me. I won't tell anyone. Anyone at all, including Ana."

"Mark, damn it, this is so upsetting to say. I can't believe it, but I think Cheryl has an alcohol problem. She may even be an alcoholic. I don't know."

"Where is she now?" I asked.

"She is in bed. She passed out. I don't know what to do. Being a lawyer does not help in this situation. Mark, what should we do? I am really frightened. I knew she drank a lot on occasion, but I didn't know it would lead to this. She has bottles hidden all around the house. I should have dealt with this matter earlier. But every time I brought the issue up, Cheryl would get mad—screaming mad. So, I just let it go. What should I do now, Mark? What in hell should I do?"

Chapter 15:
Charles

harles Yates did not like to be called Charlie. And, I mean, he really did not like to be called "Charlie."

Charles joined the social studies faculty in the fall of 1971. He was the one true political conservative in the department. We have a Libertarian, but Charles was conservative and a partisan. He was an ideological and political Republican. Charles did not budge from his principles. He was hard-core. He abhorred compromise, especially compromising with "liberals."

Whereas some teachers in Bailey High were selective with regard to which elections they voted in, Charles voted in each and every election. Some cynical faculty contended that it made little difference who was elected. They would say, "Both parties are corrupt and the people they support are corruptible, so why vote?"

Charles responded, "It does matter. We, as citizens, have an obligation to vote. I have always found one candidate preferable to others, especially the conservative candidate."

Trying to convince skeptical faculty that it did matter who got elected, Charles argued, "Conservatives govern the country better than liberals or wishy-washy moderates, so cast your vote for the conservative candidate."

Charles and I debated the question of why he held his

conservative views and what might be the implications for teaching his ideology. In one of our many conversations, Charles turned the question. "Mark, why are there so few conservatives in our department and in social studies departments elsewhere?"

"It is the nature of the beast, Charles."

"Damn it, Mark, you need to explain that to me. What do you mean?"

"Well, with the possible exception of math, business courses, and the sciences, teachers tend be more liberal. And, in political science and history that is most likely the case. Do you find something wrong with that?"

"Well, Mark, I do. If the liberal ideology enters into the classroom and affects the thinking of students, yes, then I do have a problem with it."

"Do you think it is possible to keep your views out of the classroom? Megan Straffa, for one, does not think teachers can."

"Yes. I am able to do it. Megan is wrong about that. I think I can prove it to you. I am not sure I can change Megan's mind, though. She is pretty stubborn once she arrives at a conclusion. I enjoy debating Megan —however, I am under no illusion that I can reform her extreme views. But you, Mark, I think I could change your mind because I am an unbiased teacher."

"Are you sure Charles? Besides, I am not so sure students get their political ideology from their teachers, so it may not matter. I have questioned students in the past, and except for the counter-culture types, they pretty much believe what their parents hold to be true. I believe that teachers have relatively little impact on students' political preferences. Thus, Megan believes we ought to just come out with it and let the students make up their own minds. Maybe she is right."

"I am not sure about that, although it could be that the

students' parents have had more experience and realize that conservatism is a smarter way to go. Liberal kids eventually come to their senses, especially when they have to pay the bills."

Charles continued, "So, in general, I think we need more conservatives teaching about public affairs. Therefore, the students will receive a more rational and practical education. Every once in a while we will have a teacher from the 'Troops to Teachers' program who tends to be conservative. And, sometimes a football coach will teach social studies. Some of them are conservatives but not all. Those are the only chances we have. We need more teachers who will tell kids to 'suck it up,' be more responsible, and take responsibility for their own behavior and lives. We coddle students way too much. The rest of you in our social studies department are primarily liberals. You protect students from unpleasant ideas. You shelter students from conservative concepts that might create some discomfit. Liberals are mostly about making populist statements so the populace will elect their candidates. And, you liberals don't want to say anything that might upset a student's learned biases unless those views are not the ones you favor—then you challenge them. Mark, you have to admit that yourself. You all challenge those beliefs you disagree with and accept from students those that you do agree with. What say you Mark in your own defense and that of others in our department?"

"I am not so sure I am a liberal, Charles, or anywhere near the kind of liberal you have described. You brought up the federally-funded Troops to Teachers program. Well, I always wondered why there were not 'Troops to Lawyers' or 'Troops to Physicians' programs. Veterans could also be lawyers and physicians, so why not government programs for those occupations too? I realize that some lawyers and physicians get trained in the military, but I mean a streamlined program like Troops to Teachers."

I persisted as I tried to explain to Charles how I see it, "You say that teachers tend to be liberal, but I would argue not all. I think we agree that science and math teachers tend to be less political and less liberal; although, with the earth getting hotter some environmental science educators have become activists. The study of different subjects seems to affect political leanings, although we have to watch out about over-generalizing."

"Maybe so, but the teachers I have encountered invariably tend to be liberals. I think that is too bad. I would say that is even the case for subjects other than the social sciences."

"Maybe so, Charles, but you tend to characterize anyone as liberal who is left of Attila."

We both laughed as Charles yielded a grimace.

Over the time we taught together, Charles and I would have many similar conversations. I learned through my teaching years that usually someone from Charles' background did not become a teacher. He over-rode the general rule.

Charles' father made millions in the financial industry. His mother excelled in fund raising as a volunteer for a variety of charities. Even though Charles attended public schools and a public university, he could have gone to any school or university he wanted. Indeed, his family had enough money so he could have gone to an expensive private preparatory school and then to a well-endowed private university, but he didn't.

Charles explained the reasoning: "My parents did not believe in spending money if they did not have to. Also, Mark, they had money because they didn't waste money on alcohol and tobacco like some other people." Those within earshot of Charles knew who those "other people" were he was referring to.

Charles grew up in well-funded schools in Maryland where well-heeled taxpayers made sure that the schools had the resources to garner the designation of being "good schools." The Parent Teacher Associations in the schools he attended always had money for the extra activities that schools in less wealthy areas did not have. So, going to publicly funded schools and then to the state university made economic sense to a family in which making and keeping money were important. They figured they could make it work and they did.

From the time he joined the faculty in 1971, Charles preached punctuality for his students and his colleagues. He believed, almost religiously, in structure and being on time. His students would "get sick" and leave school rather than be late for his class. If they ever walked in late, Charles greeted them with caustic commentary and what students described as "the look." Students expressed to me, "Once you were the target of the look you did not forget it or want to receive it again."

Charles' biting sarcasm could make his students shrink as they snuck out of the room when a class did not go well. Ken Lewiston induced student thoughts, Charles Yates inspected them.

With adults, Charles could also be abrasive, although he could turn on the charm and was generally well liked by his colleagues. He was a committed teacher. The faculty valued his dedication and high expectations. I liked him both personally and professionally.

Indeed, his infectious personality rendered others susceptible to his charms. Charles' well-developed persona attracted his colleagues. Yet, the same persona intimidated some of his students, but not all. A significant number of Charles' students excelled in his classes, in college, and in life. Former students came back to Bailey High and told Charles and other faculty members how much his teaching had helped them when reality set in.

Parents and students recognized Charles as an effective teacher. He lectured more than some of the rest of the teachers in Bailey High, but many of his students seemed to profit from and even relish the structure. Charles made sure that his students knew what moral and ethical behavior was. Cheating and plagiarism received a large red-inked zero or worse.

When they walked by, both Charles and his wife, Charity, turned heads beckoning the eyes of both men and women. They worked out together with weights, often with a professional trainer. At that time, rarely did anyone have a "personal trainer." Charles and Charity Yates did.

The couple hiked on weekends, watched what they ate, and drank alcoholic beverages in moderation. Charles and Charity dressed stylishly, flashed seductive smiles, attracted attention and some envy.

The Yates' did not have children. When asked: "Why no children? They would invariably respond, "It is too time-consuming and too expensive." The "too expensive" rationale did not make sense to the rest of us. Charles and Charity both came from money, and unless there was something consequential that we did not know, the married couple appeared to have more than sufficient money by combining their resources.

Charles and Charity lived in a five-bedroom house with plenty of room and a big yard in the wealthier part of town. We wondered what they did with all those bedrooms.

Charles and Charity delighted dinner parties with their travel stories. And in Bailey High, when Charles Yates and Cheryl Wattsen were in the same room at the same time, they enriched audiences with their accounts of the sights and sounds of places most of the rest of us could only dream about.

In class, Charles included in his lectures sights he had

traveled to and explored. His students remembered his class and the lessons he taught. They carried them into higher education and into their careers. I was glad to have Charles on our faculty. He offered a different perspective to our students and to the faculty.

When Charles Yates and Megan Straffa debated, which was often, their intense personalities collided and cognitive sparks flared. Those of us who watched and listened to their exchanges benefited. Charles and Megan pit their disparate perceptions of the world against each other. But discussions, in which different views can be identified and clarified, frequently lead to increased understanding. Even when their voices increased in volume and their colorful language exceeded propriety, the faculty found the Yates and Straffa intellectual melees brimming over with energy and often enlightening.

Megan's perennial opponent, Charles, did not seem to have any drawbacks or weaknesses. Megan, who had little love for conservatives, thought she could find Charles' personal flaws as well as his faulty syllogisms. She told me: "If Charles has any peccadillos, I will find them. Surely, no one is as clean as Charles appears. I think his failings are just waiting for me to uncover. Time will tell."

"Yes, Megan." I said. "Time will tell."

Charles and Megan opposed each other repeatedly over the years they worked and taught together. In their many encounters, they fiercely argued their points of view. In their arguments, and there were many, it was difficult to discern who came out on top.

Chapter 16:
Jake

*J*ake Spanner joined the social studies faculty in 1972. Politically, he was the polar opposite of Charles. Jake's liberalism permeated his being. During the period I knew him, he objected to virtually everything Presidents Richard Nixon, Ronald Reagan and anyone named Bush said, did, and stood for. Nixon and Reagan were not the same politically, but to Jake they wore the same political trousers. He wasn't much happier with the presidents who were Democrats. To Jake, the Democrats were not liberal enough.

I got to know Jake better after I became chair of the department. It became apparent immediately that he had strong political views. As the department chair, and as with Charles, I had to discuss the issue of potentially influencing his students with his political ideology. "Jake, I believe you have the right to your own views, but the students need to make up their own minds based on the evidence."

"But, Mark, I present the evidence. I let the students arrive at their respective conclusions, especially when the evidence is pretty clear."

"The evidence you present is seen through your perceptual lens. There are other ways of looking at things than the way you do. We, as teachers, should help the students see that."

"I do."

"That's not what I have observed. You are pretty good at engaging your students. I would just like to have you provide the students with alternate explanations."

"What if those other explanations are wrong? Am I still supposed to present them as factual?" I could sense the frustration in Jake's voice. He certainly did not see it the way I did.

After discussions with Megan, I now see how difficult it is to keep one's personal views out of the classroom. I have gradually become convinced that Megan has a point when she claims that teacher neutrality is not possible. Increasingly, I have come to believe that there are all kinds of ways that curricula and activity in the classroom can be slanted.

My own political views are socially liberal and fiscally conservative which puts me in the mainstream of most Americans. I do not care what people do in the privacy of their bedrooms, but I do care what public officials use my tax money for and that they do not waste it.

After further discussions with Megan and others, I came to accept that it is important for teachers to recognize that we all have biases. If we realize that we are filtering our views into the classroom and that we may be doing so unconsciously, then we may be able to acknowledge our predispositions. We could also explicitly state our biases and allow students to arrive at their own conclusions through a process of critical thinking. Megan employed this latter approach.

Further, I believe that critical thinking does not happen when teachers tell students what to think, and then hold them to those views through mandated quizzes and examinations. Teachers who talk and test to see whether the students repeat the "talk" are propagandizing at best and brainwashing in the worst cases. I believe that propagating is the antithesis to teaching.

If a teacher does state personal views, then I believe the teacher should allow students to state theirs without penalty or fear of any kind of retaliation, including a lower grade. Students then would feel free to enunciate reasons for what they assert to be true and how they arrived at their hypotheses and conclusions. If the teacher is going to take a position, the teacher ought to identify what evidence the teacher used and how that related to the position taken. Both the students and the teacher could then question each other and revise their respective notions as warranted.

Even determining the facts of a case is not easy. One story I would tell in class illustrates the point. I would use my name in the example. Here is the story: "Mr. M. went to a hotel with his secretary for a meeting and had a good time."

When the students hear the story, the students generally break out into laughter because they envision possible unbecoming behavior on the part of their highly conventional teacher. In explaining what can be learned from the story, I say, "Aha, there are important lessons for you to learn from the story. One, did you get the facts straight? Did you miss a word or two or three, such as, 'for a meeting,' which could change your interpretations of the story? And, what virtually everyone misses when I tell the story is that I never said that the secretary was a man or a woman. You probably made the assumption that it was a woman although I never said it was. An unwarranted assumption or two invariably leads to a faulty conclusion which is at odds with the truth. Did you fall for it?"

Students at this point generally realize that they had made the critical thinking error of assuming too much. And, either non-verbally or verbally admit that "Yes, we fell for it."

I then explain, "There are three important critical thinking concepts that can be gleaned from the example. First, get the facts straight; second, watch out for making assumptions; and, third, making false assumptions will inevitably lead to jumping to unwarranted conclusions. Missing any of the three maxims can get you into a heap of intellectual trouble."

At this point, the students generally get it as they learn a process of thinking that will keep them from getting caught intellectually.

As a fast learner, Jake got the point early in our interactions about teaching. He quickly realized it is critical thinking he is after rather than indoctrination. If Jake was to proselytize liberal thought in Gorham, then he was going to have a difficult time in our community with a mostly conservative school board. Furthermore, in my judgement, proselytizing is not teaching but rather is indoctrination.

Jake had graduated from a small liberal arts college where advocacy for social justice pervaded most of his classes. He bought into and accepted his professors' political leanings as liberal theory seeped through the subject matter. He read deeply and widely in political philosophy. Plato, Aristotle, Cicero, Aquinas, Peter Abelard, J. J. Rousseau, Mary Wollstonecraft, Catherine McCauley, Karl Marx, and Friedrich Nietzsche served as companions. These European-centered writers guided Jake's thinking.

Fortunately for Jake and his students, his intelligence led him to realize that in college he had mostly been reading European authors who were included in the pre-twentieth century Western canon, so he expanded his reading outside his formal education. When he read W. E. B. Du Bois, Ida B. Wells, Booker T. Washington and later Gloria J. Watkins (pen name: bell hooks), he realized that the canon in his early schooling omitted significant minority authors. He included as many as he could in his classes. His intellectual growth led him to eventually include Asian, Latino, as well as other writers from

114

around the world. This further enriched his thinking and his teaching.

When parents objected to what Mr. J. was including in his classes, he responded, "I allow my students to choose. If they want to read 'so and so,' then they can do so on their own. I don't make them read these authors, but I do let them know what they have written. It is their choice to read them or not."

Jake described in his classes what the various authors wrote about which was one way of getting around directly assigning students to read authors who wrote books that influential people in the community objected to. As a result, a number of the students read Mr. J.'s favorite authors on their own. The students became especially interested in reading Mr. J.'s favorites when he told the students that the books might be banned, "So you better read them while you still can." His caveat worked. Many of his students read the books that Jake said may no longer be available, because the censors might prohibit them. Students devoured George Orwell's *1984*, Aldous Huxley's *Brave New World*, Anthony Burgess' *A Clockwork Orange*, J. D. Salinger's *Catcher in the Rye*, Mary Shelley's *Frankenstein, The Autobiography of Malcolm X* by Malcolm X with Alex Haley, and any other book Mr. J. convinced his students might no longer be available for them to read.

As Jake told anyone who would listen, "With most censorship, the hidden eventually is uncovered, the truth emerges and students no longer listen to the censors. Censorship inevitably backfires."

Born into privilege, Jake knew he could do pretty much whatever he wanted to. Money was there for his use. He could have been a lawyer, a financial analyst, or worked in any profession where he could make a lot of money. He decided, instead, to become a teacher. His father was an attorney who had started his career as a public defender. He went into private practice to earn enough money to pay for his children's schooling.

Jake's mother stayed at home when Jake was born. His brother and his sister were already in school, so Jake had his mother's full attention. His brother, born five years before Jake, enrolled in the Peace Corp in Africa. After graduating from college, his sister, who was three years older than Jake, worked for a non-profit in Washington, D. C. Jake learned from both of them. He brought a commitment to public service into the classroom.

Students, parents, and faculty recognized Jake as a good teacher. Some of his students, however, complained that he was, in their lingo, "boring." His detractors claimed that Mr. J. would go off on tangents which drove some students up the cliché-filled wall. Some other students enjoyed the distractions that sent their minds off the immediate subject into parts unknown—a growth experience for some—ennui and irrelevance for others.

Mr. J. reached the students who came from a similar background to his, but did less well with students from a different childhood than the one he experienced. He could not understand why they didn't "care." We had discussions about what he perceived as a lack of motivation. I saw the problem as a lack of interest. I believe that it is the teacher's job to spark interest in students. Once interested, then the students motivate themselves to follow what they are passionate about.

I had professors in college who helped the classes I was in to understand young people from different backgrounds. The evidence is that schools mostly confirm the social-economic background of students. Schools tend to bestow a host of advantages onto those who have the "right" backgrounds, which translates into affirmative action for the already privileged.

The students who possess advantages and privileges get into the honors programs, the Advanced Placement courses, and are assigned what the school believes are "the best teachers." The students from such privileged backgrounds, the pre-judgments sustain, "deserve the best and are, as a result, given the best." Bias toward those who already have much is built into the system, so much so that the system finds ways to give them more and even more, including having the teachers recognized and acknowledged as the "best."

Students from low income backgrounds generally are in larger classes with the least experienced teachers. Therefore, the gap between rich and poor either stays the same or becomes wider while students are in school. In a way, schools re-educate their students into their respective socio-economic classes. Sociologists have found that once a student's socio-economic class is determined then it tends to stay that way. Contrary to the prevailing conventional wisdom, social and economic mobility is limited, even in the United States.

During my first two years of college, I did not understand the educational differences inherent in students' socio-economic-cultural backgrounds. I did not have extra money growing up, but my mother had received a small inheritance, bought and sold some land, and through various jobs made ends meet so I could continue in school. As I learned as I was teaching, some of my students' economic conditions were much worse than my own. Prior to my employment as a teacher, I had been unaware of the pre-determined fate of some of my students.

In college, I learned about the advantages of some and the disadvantages of others. When Ana and I were first married we had little to live on. My first teacher's salary was not much above the minimum wage based on the hours I put in working. So, I understood what it was like to try to provide for my family.

Yet, Ana and I were nowhere near as poor as some of the students I taught. I had always gone to school with breakfast in my belly. More than a few of my students' stomachs were growling empty when they came to school. If they did not have lunch money, or qualified for free lunch, the hunger stayed with them throughout the school day. It is difficult, if not impossible, to concentrate when one's mind and body are saturated with hunger pangs.

Jake did not seem to understand what it was like to be poor and not yet motivated to learn. I asked him, "Jake, do you know what it is like to be poor like some of your students? And, Jake, by the way, they will become motivated if you interest them. I believe it is our job to make our classes interesting, so students will be motivated to learn."

"I believe I do understand what their backgrounds are like. But, Mark, the students need to motivate themselves."

"How could you possibly know what it is like to be in their shoes? You have always had enough money to do whatever you want and buy anything your heart desired. You don't even need your teacher's salary because your parents can take care of you even if you don't work. That is not so with poor kids."

"I have read about the plight of poor people." Jake countered.

"But, reading about it is not like living it, So, Jake, I don't think you have a concrete understanding of what it is like to be without the basic necessities. I really don't believe you do get it."

"What about the parents? What is their responsibility? The parents of the kids you are talking about have to do their part, don't they?"

"Sure, they have a responsibility if they know what to do. It is hard for parents who have not been educated themselves to educate their own children. We, as their teachers, are their

118

only hope sometimes. They have to depend on us."

"Well, I think I do know how to teach all kinds of kids."

It was clear that we were getting nowhere near a meeting of the minds. We kept circling back to the same place in an argument that continued over the years we taught together in Bailey High.

I tried to move the discussion forward, "Jake, another thing. I don't think you understand those students who are yet, in your words, 'unmotivated.' You call them unmotivated but I don't think that is the problem—you think they are unmotivated and don't care about learning. As a result, they fulfill the low expectations you have for them."

"Well, if their parents cared about their children's education then they would do better in school."

"There you go again, Jake. You are back to blaming the parents again. As I already said, even if a student does have parents, their parents may be uneducated themselves and unable to help their child. Even more problematic is the fact that some of our students don't have parents, or their parents are busy earning a living so the kids will have food to eat and clothes to wear. These parents have little time for anything else, and if their parents are absent from the home for any reason, then the students often have no help from an adult."

"Well, I can't do anything about that."

"Jake, you are a funny kind of liberal. The problem Jake, as I see it, is that by the time you started to teach you had concluded that certain students did not care about their education. I believe that these students you cite as unmotivated may appear not to care, but would care if we interest them by teaching well. It is our job to help them see why they should care. Jake, you don't seem to me to quite believe that all students can get it. Do you?"

"No, Mark, if you put it that way, no I don't. They can do

something, a trade of some kind, but reach high standards? No, they can't do that."

"Jake, you and I see the world and teaching in quite different ways. I guess we will just have to agree to disagree."

Around and around we went. We would invariably end our discussions with lingering questions and significant issues remaining unresolved. We would get somewhere in our discussions because talking crystalizes the sticking points. At least after talking over our disagreements, we felt that the disputes we had were to some extent clarified. When we left each other after our discussions, we generally agreed that defining and refining the issues helped us to more precisely identify the problems. This was progress.

Jake and I kept debating and discussing teaching approaches and methods throughout our time teaching together. After each encounter, we realized we had further to go, and more discussions to have. We both felt as colleagues that there is nothing wrong with having disagreements that could be further addressed at a future time. When working with young people, answers to complex problems can be and are difficult to come by and sometimes without realistic solutions.

Some students in Jake's classes sensed their teacher's lack of confidence in their abilities. They thought that Mr. J. did not believe they could learn beyond a basic level. Teachers' preconceived notions often lead to students fulfilling what their teacher expects.

Some of the students, who were in both of our classes, confided in me that "No matter how hard I try I can't prove it to Mr. J. that I can learn what he is trying to teach." They would add, some with troubled resignation, "It is so discouraging."

And, some of the students Jake Spanner thought were not

getting what he wanted them to get tried to show him that they were learning. Some of those students met Mr. J.'s self-fulfilling expectations and fell short. Others showed him that he was wrong about them. One came back to prove it.

Chapter 17:
Karla

"Man, that woman is ditzy." I heard that in the halls over the years. I knew who they were talking about. It was Karla—Ms. K. Behind her back, in the halls when students thought no faculty were within earshot, students called her Ms. D, short for Ms. Ditz.

As the years progressed, students uttered "Ms. Ditz" as a term of endearment. In the early 1970's, men would not have been called "ditzy." Women were called that and much worse. Megan's "language lessons" were just beginning to be taught and learned, but they had not yet been comprehended and used much less instituted.

Karla Betts taught art in Bailey T. S. Memorial High School. She was nothing if not creative. We never knew what she would wear, say, or do, which made her so intriguing. I must say that I loved her, absolutely loved her, and could not wait to see her each day.

I rarely saw Karla on weekends. There were rumors as to where she could be found. I respected her privacy, valued her, and was not invited into her private life, so I never crossed into her life outside of school. Being with her in school as her friend and colleague was enthralling and rewarding enough.

In the fall of 1973, Karla joined the faculty. She had attended an art school in New York earning a Bachelor's degree in Fine Arts. She tried to make a living as an artist but had zero ability in marketing herself. She thought she might like teaching so she took the requisite number of education courses to obtain a temporary certificate to teach in a public high school. Our school had a late summer resignation so the system hired Karla Betts to teach art.

Somehow, Karla got by Mitchell Appletone's unspoken, but generally understood, "Do not hire anyone who is different" decree. The command gained additional urgency after Megan slipped through Mitchell's "Thou shall not be a non-conformist" door. The assistant superintendent, who allowed Karla into the system, may not have fully understood Mitchell's dictum.

Mitchell was on vacation when Karla was hired. After Karla's hiring while he was away, Mitchell took fewer vacations from then on until his retirement. He did not want any more like Karla employed in his school system.

Karla was, as she exclaimed ad infinitum, always on a diet. Mitchell did not like heavy women, and would comment about her weight. Men, who were overweight, like me, received a reprieve.

Because he worked out frequently, Mitchell thought he had beaten the middle age expanded middle. He had not. His affinity for donuts created a bulging roll just above his belt. Mitchell did not like to look at men who had a "beer belly," because he claimed he did not have one. He had a "donut belly" instead.

Mitchell filled his personal and professional life with a bevy of other contradictions. He had not served a day in the military, but he was military and militaristic. Mitchell, the quintessential patriot, waved flags whenever he could. Mitchell was the kind of "patriot" who voted for military intervention abroad when other families' children led the fight. His apparent guilt of not enlisting or being drafted into the service seemed to lead him into gung-ho patriotism whenever he had the opportunity. When people like Mitchell evoke patriotic fervor, I invariably think about Samuel Johnson's statement, "Patriotism is the last refuge of a scoundrel." Johnson's admonition does not indict the entire concept of patriotism, but it does critique those patriotic displays that are replete with hubris and bravado. The kind I believe Mitchell practiced.

Mitchell scolded faculty about women's dress too. He did not approve of pant suits on women, although he could not control a woman's decision to wear pants. To him, it was just not right. "It is not the way it is supposed to be," he would repeatedly say. How it was supposed to be and why it was supposed to be that way, Mitchell never said. As long as men wore a tie, were clean and neat, we got a pass on the rest of our wardrobe. No such luck for women. Mitchell's sexism flowed out of his apertures. Women felt it, sensed it, avoided it, and learned to beware of his disapproving glare because its wounds throbbed.

In the late summer of 1973, much to Mitchell's chagrin, his assistant superintendent, who was new to the system and had not yet wholly assimilated to Mitchell's ways, had interviewed Karla and offered her a one-year contract. Generally, if a new teacher performed to an unwritten set of standards, then the teacher would get another one-year contract until earning tenure, which as in Derek's case, may not protect you if Mitchell did not want it to.

We found out later that when Karla was hired Mitchell was on one of the few vacations he ever took. No one except Judy, his faithful assistant, knew where he went and when he would be back. Presumably, the school board knew where Mitchell was and when he would return, but Mitchell kept things close to his vest and controlled his list of those who "need to know."

He must have given Judy instructions that he did not want

to be interrupted on his trip. Mitchell's assistant superintendent proceeded to dutifully take care of things and signed Karla's contract. After Mitchell met Karla at an orientation session and reception, he told me that "She won't last long, probably won't last past October. After she is gone, I will replace her with a long term substitute. As you know, Mark, a long term sub to replace her would be cheaper, and, yes my dear Mark, I always like cheaper."

In one of our conversations, Karla told me about her background. "My parents had worked in the theater during my growing up and formative years. Even though I was supposed to be in school, my mother and father took me along as they moved from theater to theater. They were creative actors piecing together a living in dinner theatre along with any bit parts they could get in television or movies. I was home-schooled before homeschooling was popular. My education, Mark, until I was in the art institute was what you would call 'loosely structured.'"

Karla continued, "I had plenty of time to myself while on the road with my father and mother. The last thing I wanted to do was act in shows or act like my parents. I learned to create with the few materials or instruments of any kind that were available to me. This ability to scrounge and salvage is important for any school teacher and certainly has helped me because I work in a school district trying to get by with Mitchell as superintendent skewering the line when it comes to money for art supplies or for anything else that really matters."

Karla explained to me that the essence of art was what she called "the new," or as she defined the artistic process, "Creating ways to do things that have never been done before."

Karla stated, with an unusual air of authority for her, "The essence of the creative spirit is to see things in new ways, and then to help others see in a new way. Creativity by its very nature is to bring to life something that humans have never previously seen or experienced."

I asked, "Karla, would you consider yourself creative?"

"Yes, I guess. A lot of people think I'm weird. I guess I would agree with them. I believe you have to be at least a little bit weird to be creative. So, if being weird is necessary to be creative then I am glad I am weird."

But could Karla be creative in a public high school and survive? During her first six months as a teacher at Bailey High, the students referred to her, without affection, as "Ms. Ditz." Mitchell heard the terminology and did not like it. He could not act on it because it was not something Karla said or did. It was something said about her. It confirmed the disrespect he had for Karla. The slang uttered in his district's high school also bothered him. He could only hope that Karla would leave soon—not soon enough for Mitchell Appletone though.

First impressions are sometimes difficult to eliminate or even to mend. During those six months Karla was "Ms. Ditz," and it was not a compliment. I wondered to myself after first meeting her, "Could Karla shake the snap judgments, or did she even care?"

It took all of six months for her students to realize that Ms. K. cared deeply about each and every one of them. Her classroom became a hub, jingling with all kinds of activity and originality. She empowered students to see things previously unseen. Karla's classroom was a home away from home, and for some, a refuge. She loathed the gaudy but marveled at her students' pure creations of "beauty," her favorite word.

Surprisingly, Karla was not a soft touch for her students. She would let her students fail. She sometimes cushioned their failure so they could continue the struggle to create. She told me that "Creativity often comes out of failure, so I encourage students to keep going, just keep going. And, eventually you will create something beautiful beyond what you thought was possible or could have imagined. Sometimes what appears to be failure is but a step in the creative process. I encourage my students to continue trying—experimenting if you will."

Karla said to students, "Try again, try again. How about this? If not this, how about that? You can figure it out. You can do it. Keep going. Beauty *is* now. Beauty *is* in the process. Stay in the present and your creation will come. More beauty is just around your creative corner, but remain in the moment. Don't look ahead and you will see something beautiful right now, more will come, just ahead of you. It will come." Karla exemplified mettle.

Over the years, Karla's students won art contests throughout the state. The refrain from envious competing schools was "What are you doing there at Bailey High?" The answer was that "Ms. K. was doing here." Karla enlisted students in discovering and then exposing their creativity. When Karla's students triumphed, her entire being radiated.

Much to his dismay, Mitchell could not find a reason to make Karla leave the school system. He tried, but he could not encourage her to go. Karla was so committed to her profession and her students that she did not let the superintendent of schools trouble her or get in her way. The students came to value what she did with them and told their parents who told the school board. Mitchell, with reluctance, tolerated Karla. It was his custom to succumb to the civic will. He was, if nothing else, constantly aware of the community's political winds. Karla's innovative teaching blew her wind heartily and steadily moving her resolutely forward. She lasered through Mitchell, not bothering to go around him.

Mitchell retired from the school system in 1986. Long after Mitchell's retirement, Karla was still going strong, unfailingly seeing the world in new ways. Karla Betts outlasting Mitchell Appletone seemed to me to be a victory for rectitude, and a clear defeat for ill-informed penchants over-loaded with oxymoronic biases.

Karla humored Mitchell. She went to his retirement party in an old pantsuit. He glanced at her while she was consuming ice cream and a big piece of cake. While holding up her plate, she smiled and waved as she made eye contact with the new retiree. After Mitchell left the school system, Karla stopped dieting and lost weight.

After he retired, Mitchell stayed in Gorham. I periodically sat with him in local coffee shops. He did not seem to understand that times had changed. He told me over and over that "Things aren't the way they used to be. You know, Mark, what we need is more discipline. You know that don't you Mark?" Without waiting for my response, he ordered another donut with chocolate icing on top.

As justice would have it, after Mitchell's retired, Karla was still teaching grace by doing what she loved to do and was meant to do.

Karla taught for a long time after Mitchell departed. In his own vernacular, Mitchell Appletone was "done and gone." His sun had set.

Chapter 18:
John

ohn Browne joined the faculty in 1974. The school's enrollment had grown steadily so the school district added teachers. John was one of the new hires.

John ranks as one of the smartest and most well informed people I have ever known. From the day he joined our social studies department, I learned a great deal from him.

His father had been a middle manager in an automobile manufacturing plant in Michigan, took early retirement, moved to Massachusetts, and became a security guard.

After we got to know each other, John told me "I attended public school for a short period of time. Then I attended private elementary and secondary schools in Massachusetts. I later received a partial scholarship to attend college."

"What did your father and mother do when you were in school and did you have any brothers and sisters?" I asked.

"My father's post-retirement job as a nighttime security guard helped to pay for my schooling. He kept working until I graduated college. As for my mother, when she wasn't teaching elementary school, she stayed home with my brother, sister, and me. My brother was ten years old when my mother went to work, and my sister was eight. I was six entering first grade when mother taught full time. She retired when my brother and sister had children thinking she might be able to be an occasional substitute teacher. However, my mother stopped teaching completely in order to take care of my nieces and nephews and never returned to teaching even part time."

John was the first African American teacher at our school. Mitchell approved of John Browne's hiring warily. In one of his more candid moments, the superintendent said to me, "As long as we don't hire too many blacks who would make trouble, having one around won't hurt. The pressure is on to diversify, whatever in Hades that might mean. We might as well hire one, but I don't like it. I hope it is only one though. I will try to stop it at just one. If the feds or the state guys pressure me to hire more minorities, I won't hire any more than a few. I will string the minorities along hoping they will just go away. When the pressure is off, we will just go back to our custom of doing things my way which is also the Gorham way."

Clearly, white superiority penetrated the North as it had in the South. Bias dwelled in the minds and hearts of some of Gorham's residents, and they weren't about to change. Mitchell Appletone embodied the bigotry.

After Martin Luther King's assassination in April of 1968, "white guilt" led to more opportunities for black students in selective schools. John matriculated in an Ivy League college. John's academic background merited admission to even the most selective colleges regardless of his minority status. For minority students, being labeled an "affirmative action admit" was an insult to an accomplished student like John Browne, or any student for that matter.

The nation's preoccupation with its "guilt" soon dissipated. The hearts and minds had not changed. In some localities and colleges around the country, minority admissions and hires would be few and far between as the guilt turned into resentment to anything that smacked of affirmative action.

In my conversations with him, John seemed to have read

everything that mattered. He dotted his conversation among his colleagues with references to books and articles, along with citing relevant radio and television interviews. John read as many newspapers a day as he could find. No amount of reading seemed to satisfy his hunger to know.

"John, how did you find a way to be so well educated from a background like yours? I mean, I don't want to be or even sound patronizing, but the odds are against someone like you making it the way you have." I asked as I clumsily stuttered words filled with racial overtones and the condescension I was trying to sidestep. I was not successful in hiding my ignorance about matters of race in the United States.

"Mark, I am not offended by your questions. Keep them coming. I went to public schools first." John explained. "By the second grade, the principal told my teacher that I should be placed in the lowest grouping—the low group was called the 'Snakes.' The top students in my second grade class were called the "Swans." Not very subtle I know, but it made it clear where I and my classmates belonged, or someone in power thought we belonged. The educational deck was stacked. Looking back, it was predestined that some kids were going to win and some were going to lose."

"John, you are arguing that there are some winners and some losers, and some of it is pre-determined. In some of my college courses, the same argument was made. I discussed this issue with Jake Spanner. He doesn't see it the way I do. Please continue explaining how you see it."

"Okay. I will go further and give examples from my experience. The teacher assigned to the 'Snakes' was in her first year of teaching, so not only was I in the lowest group I had the least experienced teacher. The so-called 'smart kids,' who were in the advanced class, had the award winning teacher who had been in the school system forever and was reputed to be a stellar teacher. I had the 'one year and out' teacher. The single 'yearers,' as the students called them, would say they were leaving because they were going to change professions or start a family. These 'rookies,' as the faculty referred to the single year teachers, were placed in impossible situations teaching the largest classes with the kids labeled 'troublesome,' or 'slow.' So, the new teachers with the tough assignments just left. We introduced ourselves to a new teacher each year. Some of my friends had instability in their lives. They hoped for some stability in their school. They had trouble finding it, and the school did not provide it, especially when there were new teachers each year. Oh, also, if the new teacher was really good then the principal encouraged the teacher to stay, raised the teacher's salary, and then assigned the teacher to the Swans group the next year. It was a struggle to obtain even the remnants of an education. In a way, our school was a buffet and those of us in the Snakes group fetched the crumbs. Mark, I realize this sounds depressing, even dire, but reflecting on it now I realize how rigged the system was and still is."

"I think I see what you mean. My experience was different though. I just floated through the system. Maybe it was because I was a white guy, and in high school I played sports. Clearly your experience was different."

"Yes, my experience was different from yours, and it was different from a lot of other kids like me. Because of her teaching experience, my mother knew how to negotiate the school system. Once she recognized what was going on, she monitored my education carefully. Some kids don't have parents who are able to help their children navigate the system. I did. I fortunately had parents behind me who had my back, or I don't know what would have happened to me.

"In the so-called 'low' group, the Snakes, I soon got behind in reading. My displeased parents took out a second mortgage on our house, found a private school they thought would help me, and sent me there. It did help. My parents favored public schools and wanted me to go public, but it wasn't working for me. So, because they had the resources, I went to private school. Many of my friends did not have the same chance.

"In the private school I attended, I had some good teachers. Some of the teachers in the school had been public school teachers who were fed up with the rules in the public schools. They wanted to teach creatively, and with the smaller classes in private school, they were able to. Some of the teachers were husbands or wives of spouses who made the big bucks in their professions, so they could accept the lower salaries private schools paid because they did not really need the money, and their own kids could attend the private school they taught in with a discounted tuition. Most public school teachers, however, need the money. If they can't move to another school or profession after a year or two, they just get a second job.

"The alumni of the private school contributed generously providing for the field trips and all the other activities privates have that most public schools do not. Do you want me to go on, Mark?"

"Yes, please do." I said.

"The privates provided enormous advantages to those who could afford it. They didn't stack the deck on purpose, but the deck was stacked nonetheless. In fact, if you had money you generally went private. While I was in private school, my parents—who otherwise had a social conscience—complained about the high taxes they were paying for public schools when I was not going to them and not benefitting from them. My parents gave me an advantage over the public school kids and wanted me to keep it. It is the old cliché that is oh so true—the rich get the goodies and keep getting even more. Some of the private school parents became advocates for the public schools as long as they didn't have to pay more taxes. They became 'reformers' who wanted to change the public schools just as long as they did not have to send their own children to the publics. The terminology, 'the publics,' became shorthand for places of contempt. The hypocrites had it going for them both ways—they would appear to be advocating for the public schools while staying as far away from them as they could.

"So, Mark, I was one of the lucky ones. My parents had the ways and means to give me a chance. My parents knew what to do. Some kids don't have one parent who can help them, much less two like I had. And, even with parents, they may not know how to work the system. Mine did. I plan to send my own children, if I ever have any, to public schools if I possibly can. But, the schools are going to have to change. This 'drill and kill' for the tests is destroying kids' innate creativity. Instead, we need to hire good teachers in the public schools and then encourage them to go ahead and teach."

"I see how you negotiated and made it through the system. I agree, too, that with good teachers with the freedom and courage to teach, things could get better in our schools. Maybe you and I and our colleagues can make a difference. John, what was the college experience like for you?" I asked.

"I learned early on that you feed back to the professor what he or she gives you. Most professors don't like disagreement even when they say they do, but from my experience they really don't. I just fed back to the professor what he or she fed me in class. That way, I received a lot of A's and B's.

"In some of my classes, the professors conversed with themselves. They called it a lecture. The lecturing professors just stood up and deposited information into the heads of trusting students. Professorial pontificating left little room for student thought, much less critical thinking. The lecturers just transported their personal knowledge, and I emphasize

THEIR, into their students' heads. Instead of getting to know their students so they could tailor their narratives to their students, these lectors tailored their comments to themselves. I and my classmates joked that we could have walked out of the room and the professor would just keep on talking. Generally, no one was listening. We didn't walk out. We just stopped going to class, except, of course, for the exams.

"As long as you did what the professors told you to do, you would be alright. I and many of my fellow students learned that lesson early. I did have some good teachers. Some of them were even great. However, in college, there seemed to be a prejudice among the faculty against 'popular' teachers. Some senior professors apparently thought that popular teachers must be that way because they were 'grade inflators.' It was the kiss of death to be considered 'easy.' Those junior professors who were thought of as being 'too easy' were, in most cases, eased out prior to being tenured."

"Geesus John, I never thought of it the way you describe it. Thinking back, though, there was a lot of the professor talking and the student listening where I went to school. Not much of it stuck. In order to teach history, I had to learn it—almost all of it for the first time."

"Well, Mark, think further. You are a privileged white guy, not a rich one but privileged nonetheless. I am glad you get what I am saying. However, I see it through the eyes of someone who was not in the group that was on top. I have had to look at it from the bottom up. You were at least somewhere in the middle. I and my friends started in the bottom. Most stayed there. My parents were able to help me escape, but I was just one out of many. I got an education. Most of my associates did not.

"Most of the education I got in college though was outside the classroom. I had to claim an education. You and I did much the same thing. We got our education outside the classroom, but we had the advantage of being in a college environment where we could find our way. Most of my neighbors did not get the opportunity we did."

"John, you may be right about the white privilege thing, although my instinct is to become defensive. I want you to keep helping me to see how you see it. But, if you have the system figured out, why do you work so hard? You could simply manipulate the system instead."

"I always feel like I have to catch up, like I have something to prove. And, I don't think I have it figured out. I am still learning how to survive. But now that I have found out how meaningful and fun learning is—I want to do a whole lot more of it. I have concluded that learning will liberate me and others. That is why I am a teacher. I am learning as I teach and I want to help others learn through my work as a teacher. I hope someday to go back to my old neighborhood and teach there."

"Yet, John, you said you have something to prove. Is this still the case after what you have accomplished?"

" Yes, Mark, I realize that some people do not believe black intellectual capacity is up to speed with white folk. I set out to prove that particular bias to be the myth it is. I throw the bigots a curve, in part, because I don't fit the stereotype of an 'angry black man.' They have to think about what I am up to, which is nothing more than being a good teacher and citizen."

My colleagues and I wondered if John ever slept. In his classes, students got used to his constantly recommending books they should read. Students quoted him as saying, "These are the authors you should know about. You should understand and comprehend what they have written." The students soon forgot, at least while in his class, that John's skin was a different color than theirs. He was a teacher in the best sense of the word. Students knew he was different but it soon didn't matter.

Because we already had a Mr. J., the students asked, "What should we call you?"

John turned it back to the students, "What do you want to call me?"

They asked, "Can we call you Mr. J. O.?" John liked the rhythm of the J affixed to the O. So, from then on, Mr. J. O. it was.

When John relaxed, which was not often because he thought he had to always be on, he could rap with the best of them. His students would periodically ask him if he would rap part of a lesson. He did not want to be labeled a "rapper," but occasionally he rolled into cadence. John always had a point to make. The rapping helped to make it.

The students would leave the class and exclaim how "cool" that part of the class was, as they rapped their way down the hall to the next class. The students respected John enough to stop rhyming once they got to another teacher's classroom door. They didn't want to get their teacher in trouble. They had fun in Mr. J. O.'s class, learned a lot, and appreciated how their teacher was trying to help them learn.

Even though John was not from the "street," he knew of the street. "I am fully aware of where I came from and that it is an environment a world apart from what my less fortunate 'brothers and sisters' experience in the city, the suburbs, the exurbs, and in rural areas day in and day out. I am fortunate that my wide and deep reading and my own experiences help me to understand some things and realize that I did not live the lives of those less fortunate than I. So, I know that I do not totally comprehend what some others live through, because I have not lived it."

A noose that was placed on John's car windshield one hot August day led him to realize that the prejudice in some parts of Massachusetts was not that different from the more segregated South. In some ways, the bigotry was worse because of the temptation to expect more in "Union" territory. John said to me, "I believe the symbols of cultural superiority and stares of pre-judgment are as penetrating in the North as what I have experienced when visiting relatives in the South."

We both wondered who placed the noose on John's car. I asked him, "Who in Gorham would do such a thing?"

"I am not so sure the perpetrator is from Gorham. It could be someone from anywhere in our midst. For example, the so-called liberals look at me as if I soothe their prejudices, of course, as long as I don't get too close. This past summer, I went to a town in New England for a Fourth of July celebration. The residents stared at me as if I were from another planet, Mark, no, they glared at me as an invader from another galaxy. Very uncomfortable and uninviting, and this was in so-called 'liberal' Massachusetts. Except for me, everyone at the Independence Day parade was white. A white-sheeted Ku Klux Klan march could not be any whiter. You would think the North is different. It really isn't. I got the message. I was out of town by the time the sun went down. Sundown towns aren't only in other parts of the country. New England has its share. When I go to various places in New England, the residents stare at me with half smiles on their faces. I get the vibes the message those 'smiling faces' are conveying to me—GO AWAY! That is what I detect anyway. Mark, it is a very uncomfortable feeling. Very uncomfortable, indeed."

"John, maybe you are overreacting."

"No, Mark, I don't think so. Besides, I am telling you what it feels like to me. Of course, you northerners would never say a racist thing to my face. But that doesn't mean people up here don't think it."

Once I got to know John, and we developed a semblance of

trust between us, he expressed more of his unguarded perceptions. I am under no illusions that John disclosed all his candid thoughts because John did not fully trust anyone, but occasionally John did share some of his unvarnished observations. In one conversation, he told me, "Mark, I know that to most bigots 'Negra' and 'Negro' are variations of the same theme—hate. Smiling faces cannot occlude the ingrained advantages inherent in white privilege. I and other African Americans like me are fully aware that we are often presumed incompetent until we prove otherwise. Even then, for some people, demonstrated competence is not enough because the fact of color runs deep in the hearts and minds of those who prejudge."

And, then, to lessen the tension, he added, "Oh, yah, Mark, I am no good at playing basketball, so that stereotype has to go. On the other hand, I do play a mean game of chess. Want to play?"

John said that he recognized early that "My classroom is de facto segregated. The system tries to fool us. The people in power frequently segregate under the guise of 'honors' and 'gifted.' These classrooms are divided along socio-economic lines. The kids from wealthy backgrounds are in the gifted and talented classrooms. We relegate the low income students to the lower groups. Every once in a while, a 'disadvantaged' student will 'sneak' into the classes of the privileged. Then the school system boasts about how good we are because 'Don't you see— anyone can make it.' Not so. Minority and low income students making it are the exception to the rule. Then when we do, the head 'masters' parade us out on stage, and say, 'Look how liberal we are. We even allow black kids to succeed.' I know this sounds bitter, Mark, but you asked for the truth about the way I see it."

John was on a roll and continued, "It just so happens that

black and low-income go together. I realize that there are a lot of poor white folks. Mark, I do. However, African American history has been different. We have lived through centuries-long enslavement where it was against the law to be taught to read. Then there were the Jim Crow laws and Black Codes, followed by Plessy v. Ferguson which solidified unequal segregation, and more recently we have seen re-segregation through special education classes and the gifted and talented selection process. When I bring such things up, I hear in the background the 'angry black man comments.' But studies indicate that, with some exceptions, families with higher incomes have children who score better on tests and have higher grades than those who are from families with lower incomes. Income inequality and test scores are correlated—not race—it is income. On the other hand, because of historical antecedents in this country, in general, low income and race go together. In fact, the environment surrounding low income families may be directly related to underachievement in school—therefore, a culture has been inflicted on us in which there is little hope for success leading to and maybe even causing the hopelessness some poor kids feel. Mark, as you can see, it is income inequality that divides us all. In addition, our housing patterns further confine us into impoverished neighborhoods. The controlling elite zone us into poverty interacting with poverty."

John articulated further, "The school system uses lower test scores from culturally biased standardized exams to justify the 'homogeneous' grouping in classes. The so-called 'best' teachers teach the classes with the 'brighter' students while the students in the 'lower' classes have the least experienced and presumably least able teachers. This further exacerbates the gap. Privileged folks think that there is a gap because they are just plain smarter. I beg to differ. Wealthier kids get more advantages than do children who do not have the resources. It is the circumstances you are born into that make the difference, not the fact of who you are."

In our faculty meetings, John convinced most of the faculty that the deck was stacked against students from backgrounds where there were fewer opportunities. Through the tracking system in schools, the students from the lower economic neighborhoods had their status confirmed rather than moved higher. John believed this was wrong. Furthermore, he argued, "Schools frequently conflate poverty into academic disadvantage confirming social economic status as a predictor of how well someone does in school. Mark, that is not fair or right."

The noose incident really got to John, but he had no place to go or to move to. Nor, as he expressed, could he show his anger. "Mark, if I show how much the noose episode bothers me, then the racists dismiss me as 'an angry black man.' I have to find other ways to deal with the racism."

John was mature enough to realize that moving might not change anything except his location. John could not change his color nor did he want to. He could not forget that he was black even for a moment, and people would not let him. John did not want to go away but he wished that people prejudging him and his brothers and sisters based on the color of one's skin would go away. For John, and others like him, prejudice salted long-lasting wounds.

Invisible bigotry is difficult to confront because it is seldom apparent. The bigot misses racism's deep-seated injury that it causes—never to disappear. Bias is culturally dependent relying on single mindedness. It is always there—hovering in the shadows. John knew it was ubiquitous. He could touch the unseen but palpable hate.

John said in an informal meeting with me and other faculty

that "Denial will not get racism to go way. Recognition that there is a problem will at least get us to talk about the issues. Some white people say there is not a problem that needs to be confronted. There is a problem. It cannot be wished away."

In the meeting, Megan Sraffa responded, "Yup. I know what you mean John. Women of all colors are often invisible too. And, God-forbid, that we should show our anger about it. People try to hide the racism and sexism. They believe that hiding racism and sexism makes it vanish. But we know it is there. I feel it. And, John has expressed that he feels it."

Indeed, for John, the unheard racism residing in society's alcoves did not need to have the slanders spoken. The slights were all around him in Gorham and elsewhere, submerged sometimes, but omnipresent nonetheless. John bristled silently because, "Taking the issues inherent in institutional racism and its resulting personal manifestations to the public might cause more hurt for me as well as for those who are outed. But, maybe I will have to do it."

When John Browne walked into Gorham's stores, and was not recognized as a Bailey High teacher, clerks watched to see if he was buying or stealing. This galled John. He understood the behavior was rooted in stereotypes. Understanding helped somewhat. Yet, the constant surveillance and pre-judgments of what he might do and who he might be really pissed him off.

Chapter 19:
Zackeri

*D*erek Randallston resigned in April of 1975. We needed a temporary but capable replacement. With just two months until the school year ended, the school district wanted to employ a substitute to cover Derek's classes for the rest of the year while we began a search for a permanent social studies teacher for the next year.

We found Yvonne Beane who stepped in to teach until the school year ended in June. The faculty liked her well enough to recommend her for the position for the next year. However, she was on her way to another job outside of education. Thus, we undertook a search to find a permanent social studies teacher to replace Derek.

We interviewed candidates during the summer. We again found someone we wanted to hire, Zackeri Barber. We offered him a job and he took it. Going into the fall semester of 1975, we would now have a full complement of social studies teachers.

Zackeri preferred being called Zack. He liked the spelling of his name but became frustrated trying to spell it for everyone. When introducing himself, he would politely say, "Just call me Zack. Spelled, Z-A-C-K, thanks."

Zack, like me, had two children, so any extra money he earned was helpful. He had a background in athletics. Our district could pay him an extra $800.00 to be an assistant basketball coach for two teams. Zack took the job as a social studies teacher and an assistant basketball coach.

The basketball teams needed the help. Bailey High was a perennial football power, but the basketball teams generally had losing records. Zack was assigned to assist both the girls and boys teams. They shared the gym for practice and played their games back to back. Zack agreed to the dual assignment. Thus, Superintendent Mitchell Appletone maneuvered a way to hire one coach for two teams for one stipend.

The stipend for each of the football team's assistant coaches was $2500.00 to coach one team. At Bailey Memorial, football was big. All too frequently, football over-shadowed everything else at the school.

I served as a jayvee basketball coach for a couple years while Zack was an assistant to the varsity teams. I got to know him as a coach and as a teacher which helped me to understand and appreciate him as a person. I soon became aware that I could learn a lot about a colleague within the walls of a gymnasium. Coaching also gave me a chance to know some of my students better by interacting with them outside of a classroom.

Zack introduced libertarianism to our staff. Zack was an ideologue, not a partisan. His colleague, Charles Yates, was a partisan but not an ideologue. That was the difference between the two, and it was huge.

Zack did not like liberals or conservatives—Republicans or Democrats. "I am for freedom and that is it." Zack did not rant— he announced.

Jake Spanner, an avowed liberal, seldom found government assistance he did not like. Zack, on the other hand, did not find many governmental decisions he did like. Jake and Zack were political opposites. Yet, in regard to some legislative decisions and public policies they came to the same conclusions. Liberals and libertarians often meet on the other side of the political curve—they often sleep in the same civic bed.

In one of our informal discussions, Zack said, "I find conservatives to be hypocrites. They say they favor the 'Ds': Deficit reduction, Debt control, and Defense. But they favor spending so much on defense that it breaks the budget." Then with sarcasm, he added, "So much for controlling the debt and deficits."

Zack continued, "The 'bleeding heart' liberals, on the other hand, are primarily concerned with the 'Es'—Equity in Education, Equality in the socio-economic society, and the Environment, all of which tend to create deficits and debt. The Democrats might also be for controlling spending but they don't say so very loudly. However, as their argument goes, Democrats claim that spending on the 'Es' can improve society and eventually reduce the costs associated with poverty and imprisonment, which they argue result from a lack of education. I do not think there is any proof to support that argument. My view is that the only thing that really matters is freedom—freedom of choice."

"How about defending our country?" I asked.

"I want just enough defense spending to protect the United States. We should stay out of other nations' business. We should defend ourselves, our borders, and our freedoms. Other than that I want the government to stay out of the affairs of liberty-loving Americans." Zack's political philosophy was pretty clear. He was not reluctant to enunciate it.

Zack grew up in a town where "urban renewal" had changed his neighborhood and demolished his childhood home. In one of our early conversations, I asked Zack, "What happened in your community? You are obviously bitter about what the government did."

Without hesitating, Zack responded, "Well, in the late 1960's, the United States government thought it could improve the cities by knocking down neighborhoods. The town's officials called it 'Urban Renewal.' So, the 'renewers' came in with their bulldozers, destroyed homes, and eliminated neighborhoods. The government destroyed my parents' home near Chicago under the guise of improving neighborhoods by gutting them. Then the government, in its infinite wisdom, put our land out for sale to the highest bidder. Fat cats from out of town came in, bought a resident's land for a pittance, used eminent domain to take people's homes, then the developers built condos, restaurants, stores, and hotels. They made a mint. We were paid a meager amount for our homestead. I have been against government intervention of almost any kind ever since. Government invariably takes from the poor and middle class and gives to the rich. Government is filled with a bunch of greedy elected public officials feeding a plethora of greedy developers who in turn contribute to political campaigns so the obedient political candidates can get re-elected. Then the vicious cycle goes round and round. I say, Fuck 'em."

"I see you feel strongly about this Zack." I said with obvious irony. "Government does some good though, doesn't it?"

"Sorry, Mark, other than defense I can't think of any."

"Government establishes public schools. Aren't the schools a good thing for the general public? And, Zack, how do you plan to educate your own children?

"It depends on how you look at what the public schools do. Education is a good thing, but government control of what happens in schools is not the way to go, in my judgment. I plan to homeschool my kids."

"Zack, explain that to me further. I'm not sure I get what you are saying. I need you to make your point clearer."

"The state controls the curriculum, how we instruct

students, how the students are assessed, and the government controls who graduates and who doesn't. That is a lot of power. Historically, the public schools have been used to controlling students so they will be 'good little boys and girls,' and then when they grow up they will be obedient sheep-like citizens feeding at the public trough."

"This begs the question, Zack, why are you teaching in a public school?"

"That is easy to answer. I have two kids and a wife. I needed a job. You, as chair of the social studies department, seemed like a nice guy. You assured me that as long as I give kids a chance to make up their own minds that I would have freedom in the classroom. I am not out to make 'little libertarians.' I am more than willing to let students think for themselves. Besides, I love coaching basketball, needed the extra money as a coach, so I took the job coaching and teaching. That was a pretty good rationale for me to take the job. Furthermore, there did not appear to be any reason to turn down the opportunity of teaching and coaching at Bailey High. So, here I am, for better or worse. I hope for the better for all of us."

"Okay. That makes sense. As a father myself, with your philosophy regarding life and education, I was wondering how are you going to educate your children. You said you are going to homeschool your kids."

"Yah, that's what Jennie and I are thinking of at this point. Jennie will take the lead on homeschooling. We don't like the government using our kids as human capital in their goal of making money for rich people. We believe in freedom—letting people make their own decisions and that goes for our children."

When he was going to school, Zack's parents both had jobs that scraped against the minimum wage. His mother waited on tables looking for the next tip. His father took care of various industrial plants serving as a custodian. When their home near Chicago, Illinois, was taken for urban renewal, they rented affordable apartments in Chicago's suburbs.

Zack's vigorous response to the government's use of eminent domain in order to, as Zack said, "Confiscate my parent's property and rout them out of their homes," demonstrated his strong feelings about government intervention into the lives of citizens. "Those bastards" he said, "they took my parent's home, a home my Mom and Dad loved and could walk back to from shopping and their friends' homes. The government paid my parents a portion of its actual worth. My parents had to move away from their life-long friends in a neighborhood where they sat on the front steps at night talking with people as they walked by. My parents felt safe there. The government forced my parents to leave a place they called home to go to a place that was foreign to them. The government took their freedom away. Mark, you can see why I am a Libertarian and want to get the government off the backs of the American people. Don't you?"

Zack attended a state university because it was low in cost. He lived six miles away so he was able to commute to school. He did not own a car, so he hitched rides with friends who were also attending the university. He recounted, "I received an okay education there. Too many liberal professors, though. I bought the propaganda while I was a student. Besides, buying it led to good grades. When I got out in the real world, and was able to think for myself, I rejected a lot of the crap I had been fed in college."

Because he had been a good student in high school, and then successful academically in college, Zack found time to play intramural sports, especially basketball. He graduated on time, married his high school sweetheart the day after his college graduation, and had two children during the couple's first three years of marriage. Zack and Jennie enjoyed little time to themselves after a weekend honeymoon.

Zack prided himself on keeping his hair fashionably shaggy. "Jennie likes it this way and so do I. I must admit that I see it as a freedom thing to have my hair any way I want." He said. "Employers sometimes have a problem with it. When I interviewed for this job, I cut my hair a little and combed it. I got the job. Then I let the shag grow back."

Explaining further his reasons for teaching, Zack said, "I looked into various jobs before settling on teaching. I investigated private schools for employment, but soon realized that my family and I couldn't live on the salary private schools were able to offer. Jennie wasn't working outside the home, so I needed to make more money. The job at Bailey High paid more, provided an opportunity to coach basketball which I love, so I was willing to give it a try.

"I am by nature a critic. As you know, Mark, I am critical of public education, but I am also critical of private education." Zack went on, "The escape to private schools is an elitist effort to avoid us commoners—you know—the common people like us. During colonial times, the rulers called the commoners the 'meaner sort,' which was meant to ridicule and demean. Even today, we call some of our students, 'at risk.' How would we like to have our kids, Mark, called at risk? The terminology at risk degrades a young person—at risk for what?" Zack said with a wink, but a serious one.

"The elite deny what I have said is the case, but the elite can send their children to private schools because they have money. And, with some of the parents who send their kids to private institutions, it is a way to stave off any significant integration with those who are different. If a student is a minority and comes from money, then 'it is okay' for them to mix with the primarily white privileged class. Of course, as long as there are not too many of 'those people' integrating 'their' schools, then the 'better sort' can find it tolerable."

Zack, the Libertarian, spared no one when it came to his critical, cynical eye. His intellectual arrows had a zing to them as they splintered targets. He aimed barbs at me now and then. I never asked him what he thought of me or my teaching. I did not want to know. Zack was just the kind of person who would tell me what he thought. Such truth tellers are frightening to those of us who sometimes, and for some things, do not want to hear it. When Zackeri Barber joined the Bailey T. S. Memorial High School faculty in August of 1975, he was ready to tell us what he thought—the unadorned truth as he saw it. We needed to be ready because Zack was going to fling it at us whether we were ready or not.

Chapter 20:
"Potluck"

*O*ur first Friday night potluck dinner occurred on October 26, 1973. Megan Straffa, Ken Lewiston, Cheryl Wattsen, Charles Yates, Jake Spanner, Derek Randallston, and Karla Betts attended along with Ana and me. As the hosts, Ana and I provided the basic utensils for dining. Each teacher brought either a main dish, salad, dessert or something to drink. If I had been on a diet, the Friday potlucks were a time in which it would have been broken. I ate my share of desserts. I should have avoided them all together but did not. That pesky weight problem of mine persisted and was not about to go away.

Ana and I hoped that these dinner meetings might allow us and our colleagues the opportunity and time to discuss personal, professional, school, as well as national and international issues. We speculated that such discussions could help us each personally and provide an avenue for us to dissect some of the problems and opportunities we faced in our respective classrooms. Conceivably, these exchanges would enable us to develop effective strategies to guide our lives and our work as teachers.

I thought that during our potluck dinners that if there were no compelling political or world events that we needed to discuss that we would take up personal and school issues first.

However, an event of profound national and even international political importance materialized on Saturday, October 20, 1973. Newspapers throughout the United States and many in the world reported the events in the next day's Sunday newspapers.

We agreed before we started our discussions that we would keep our deliberations private and out of the school. We realized that many of our comments probably would be personal. Others could be construed as political and critical of the school. Our views might also be taken out of context. Besides, we wanted to be candid and open with each other without fear of retribution—personal or professional.

We lived and worked in a community where politics and religion were generally avoided in "polite company," which is one way to keep things from changing. However, we prepared to discuss the political and the religious—plus whatever else came up.

This first session was six days after what was dubbed "The Saturday Night Massacre." Because of the importance of the issue, we had decided to skip introductions because we already knew each other. We anticipated knowing more about each other and what we each believed through our discussions which we hoped would continue during our occasional Friday night potlucks.

The "Saturday Night Massacre" was a major event in October of 1973. What happened on that Saturday night reached deep into America's political soul. It had far-reaching and profound national and international implications.

Because of the political import of the "Massacre," and President Richard Nixon's firing of the Special Prosecutor who was looking into the Watergate case, we needed to make sure we had as many facts straight as we could. Class discussions would surely follow and needed to be based on evidence. Many in our community were Republicans who defended Nixon against what they thought were political attacks by the Democrats and a "liberal" media.

Two federal administration officials who protested the dismissal of Special Prosecutor Archibald Cox resigned. They contended that Cox's firing transpired without cause. Our first potluck agenda proposed discussing that political event and its possible aftermath as our main issue.

Even though I had planned to start our potluck discussion this evening focusing on the Watergate crisis, the plan was soon halted. After we fetched something to drink, I asked, "Any comments about what has been called the "Saturday Night Massacre"?

It soon became apparent that we had more pressing school-related concerns to address. Before anyone could respond, Megan brought up a more immediate problem. She said, "Whoa, we can't go there yet. National affairs will have to wait. There is something happening in our school that we need to talk about first and try to find a solution." Megan made it clear that school-related issues would come before political discussions in our Friday potluck dinners. This made sense to the rest of us. Our eyes moved to Megan.

With a sense of urgency, Megan said, "I have this student in one of my classes, Crissy, who has been bullied to the point where she talked to me about dropping out of school. Is there anything we can do?"

"What has been happening to her?" Ken inquired.

Megan responded, "I found Crissy crying on Wednesday. I asked her what was happening. She told me that some girls have been following her into the bathroom, and then when she sits on the toilet they force the door open and slap her and punch her in the face."

"Ouch." Karla blurted.

"That isn't all. On Friday, Crissy told me that these same girls pulled her by her hair and put her head into another toilet where there were feces in the bowl. Disgusting, I know, but that is what she told me happened."

"I thought only guys did those kinds of things," Cheryl interjected half-jokingly breaking the tension momentarily.

Ana, who feels deeply about every human being, smarts when she hears of young people being bullied said, "Is there anything we can do Megan? This is just awful."

I, too, was disturbed and wondered what we could do about this. I asked "Does the principal know about this?"

"Probably not—and even if he did it wouldn't do any good. He is a wuss," said Cheryl.

"You are probably right Cheryl. Even though the principal ought to know, it wouldn't do any good and might make matters worse. We are required to report to the social services agencies in town what happened, but we can do that directly without going through the principal."

The "wuss" Cheryl was talking about was our principal, Ralph Giffin, who liked to be called "Sir." He had arrived as principal of Bailey High in the fall of 1972. Mr. R. was part of the first "accountability movement." Periodically, "reformers," like "Sir Ralph," are hired to make things "right." They expect us to genuflect as they attempt to make teachers more accountable. Many of these so-called reformers have never spent a day as a teacher in any classroom, kindergarten through high school. They think they "know" what needs to be done. In actuality, most don't have a clue. Ralph Giffin was a quintessential specimen of cluelessness.

I frequently complained to Ana, "Ralph has no teaching experience, although he had been a tutor—big deal. The idea of a businessman running Bailey High excited Mitchell. Ralph did have an MBA which gave Mitchell enough reason to hire him. Mitchell must have gathered that Ralph would make the trains go on time even if the trains had no one in them and no place to go. Even though Ralph had never been a full-time classroom teacher, Mitchell was able to use his connections to get Ralph appointed as a principal, albeit with temporary certification.

"Ralph and Mitchell are a match made in the educational underworld. They agreed that every dollar counted. However, in his stinginess to please Mitchell, Ralph eschewed the educational needs of students."

Ana listened patiently to my 'Ralph rants' without responding. She knew that I didn't like or respect my principal or my superintendent.

"Ana, furthermore, Mitchell's theory behind Ralph's hiring was that schools needed to be run like businesses; thus, according to Mitchell, a person trained in business is the right person for the job. Wrong! Ana, Ralph does keep expenses down. But it is a disaster for the education of students.

"Ralph cut the budget items that would have helped students to go on field trips, enjoy after school activities, have individualized tutoring, experience theatrical performances, and enable us to purchase innovative instructional materials. Ralph believes that traditional textbooks are okay as long as there is nothing controversial in them. Damn it, Ana, as you can see I am not happy about businessmen, who are not educators, running schools as if the kids are products. To these business guys, and they are mostly guys, everything is all about money. I know I said it before, but damn it!"

Ralph protected the sports programs from any budget cuts because he believed competing in high school was a business-like activity, and Ralph was all about business. Besides, cutting sports would have the community up in arms especially in a big sports' district like ours. Eliminating teachers or staff did not stir the same kind of a community furor. Even in Gorham's difficult financial years, the sports programs experienced increases in their budgets—never a decrease. The academic program had no such luck.

Ralph had no idea of how to relate to students, teachers or parents. On the other hand, he was good at relating to business men, with the emphasis on MEN. Ralph and the business community spoke the same language, shibboleths for all.

Even though Ralph fathered four children, he seemed to possess little sense of the issues facing young people. As with Mitchell, he must have never let his wife out of the house because no one ever saw her in the three years Ralph was principal at the school. For better or worse, he was our principal from the fall of 1972 through the spring of 1975.

Mitchell Appletone loved having Ralph as the high school principal, because the superintendent controlled Ralph. When Derek was told to leave, I told him he had to go. Mitchell by-passed Ralph entirely even though he was principal of the school and should have been the person to tell a teacher that he was through.

Ralph left the school in June of 1975 to return to the financial industry where he could use his self-important, unctuous character to make enough money, as he said, "To provide for my family."

When I heard Ralph Giffin resigned from Bailey High to make money, I exclaimed as loud as I dared that he did all he could to "save" money by keeping teachers' salaries down, "How about us? We want to support our families too."

Yet, in the real world Ralph was still our principal in the fall of 1973 when Megan told us about Crissy. The idea of having a principal who knew nothing about education, except that which he experienced as a student, really irritated, exasperated, and annoyed me and some of my colleagues.

Ralph had never studied education nor had he taught; however, he had the authority to tell us what to do.

So, on that evening when we were trying to find a way to help Crissy's situation we believed that Mr. R., our businessman principal, would be of no help. He understood numbers but people were not numbers and he did not understand people. To the "bean counters," like Ralph, students are data points.

The potluck group agreed that even telling Ralph could backfire, although he, as principal of the school, needed to know. He might tell us, 'I will take care of it," and he either would do too little or too much. So, we believed that we— the teachers in the school— had to do something. We just didn't know what.

We ended the discussion concerning the bullying abuse of Crissy with nowhere to turn except to be aware, vigilant, understanding, and kind to her. Possibly not much of a solution but the only one we could come up with.

Megan reported the incident to social services in our community. She left it with the agency to decide how and what to convey to Bailey High's principal as required. Ralph would not be angry that we went around him. He would only be dismayed if a report of the incident got out of the school and Mitchell heard about it. This principal smothered information that he did not like. Sir Ralph controlled our school by limiting transparency. When he could, he choked the revelation of unpleasant news.

Toward the end of dinner, we moved on to President Nixon's firing of Archibald Cox. I started the discussion with the facts as we thought we knew them. "President Nixon fired the Special Prosecutor Archibald Cox who was looking into the break-in at the Watergate Hotel that had erupted as a national news story in June of 1973. Mr. Cox asked the president for audio tapes of conversations in the White House. Nixon refused."

The existence of the audio-tapes had been revealed during the hearings before a United States Senate Committee. The president rejected Cox's request for the tapes. Nixon then fired Special Prosecutor Cox. The Attorney General, Elliot Richardson, resigned in protest to the firing as did his Deputy, William Ruckelshaus. The firing of Cox and the resignations have been called "The Saturday Night Massacre." I asked the potluck group, "What do any of you think about the situation and how we should teach about it?"

Derek jumped in immediately, sarcastically understating what he really thought, "I believe he, Nixon, is in some kind of big dung, or should I say trouble."

"What kind of trouble are you thinking Derek?" Ken asked, not buying into Derek's sarcasm.

"Impeachment-type trouble." Derek characteristically used sarcastic understatements at first but then became more direct. He was being direct now.

"Oh come on Derek. There is really nothing to this. The media don't like Nixon. The liberals on television and in the newspapers are making much about nothing." Charles said adding his viewpoint to the discussion.

"I agree with Derek." Jake said.

"I am shocked, Jake, that you would side with another liberal." Charles said with bogus sincerity.

"You guys are ganging up on Nixon and Charles. Don't we have to wait until all the facts come in?" Cheryl said.

Megan couldn't hold back and said, "Nixon is a male chauvinist in addition to being 'a tricky Dick.' Charles, you are always defending Nixon. He SHOULD be impeached!"

Ken came back, "Megan, being a male chauvinist should have nothing to do with it. Is Nixon a crook? That is the question."

"Well chauvinism should and does matter. It shows what kind of a man he is, Ken. Nixon is a bully. He tried to bully Cox, and when he couldn't bully him he fired him. And, I repeat, he is a chauvinist."

Derek added quickly, "Yup, I agree. Nixon is a crook and a chauvinist."

Ken, with his usual calm demeanor said, "The charge of 'high crimes and misdemeanors' is a high bar to reach in order to convict a president. James Madison and others at the Constitutional Convention of 1787 wanted to make it difficult to remove a president. It can't be just a political disagreement, even a serious one. It has to be a crime against the country. Did Nixon commit a crime is the question?"

"Damn it, Ken, you always deflate our exaggerated biases with facts." Megan said with a chuckle.

"Even so, I agree that Nixon is guilty." Jake said.

"You would Jake. You are one of those liberals with biases that I have mentioned to Mark and anyone who would listen to my point about the dominance of liberals in social studies classrooms. Jake, I don't think you have ever met a conservative you like. I hope you don't bring your biases into the classroom although my guess is that you do."

"I don't Charles, at least any more than you do."

"According to you and Megan, conservatives can never be right. Can they?" Charles added.

"Oh, poor Charles, everyone's picking on the conservatives. The conservatives run this country." Megan said.

"Megan, are you trying to piss me off? If so, it is working."

Cheryl nudged the discussion back to the issue. "I agree with Charles. I don't think we have enough evidence yet to convict a president of serious crimes. We need to wait and see. As I said before, the facts aren't all in."

Charles looked at me, "Okay, Mark, what do we do in discussing the issue with our classes when school begins next week?"

"I don't know." I said. "In any event, we need to be ready to present the issue to our students when we get to school on Monday."

"We cannot just assume the president is guilty of something. We have to present all the sides." Charles declared.

"I agree with Charles, and with Cheryl that we don't know enough yet. We have to present both sides until we find out what the truth is. Assuming things before we know more can get us into an intellectual quagmire that we can't easily get out of." Ken said.

"Well, how do we present both sides to students? It is truth versus lies as far as I am concerned." Derek's sarcasm surfaced again.

"Damn it Derek. Your biases have led you to assume guilt." Charles retorted.

Before we could get any further trying to figure out what we should be doing in teaching about the Watergate break in, Megan received a call. She had told a friend where she would be in case she needed to be reached.

Megan took the call. Her face turned ashen. "Are you sure?" She said. "I will be right there."

Megan grabbed her coat and got ready to go as she told us about the call. "Crissy's mother is in a panic. Crissy left a note that she was going to find another place to live. She told her mother she couldn't stand being teased and bullied anymore. I am going to her house right now to see if I can help her mother find Crissy."

"Can I go with you?" I asked.

Megan usually rebuffed offers of help but this time she did not even hesitate and said, "Yes, Mark, that would be good. I am pretty upset. Depending on what we find out, I may need support. Thank you." A vulnerable Megan was not something I, or any of us, were used to seeing or had experienced very frequently.

As often happens with teachers, just when you think you know what you are going to do on Monday, an event or crisis like Crissy's intercedes. Teenagers change daily, indeed, momentarily. Once a teacher thinks a problem is solved another one surfaces, sometimes more than one.

"So, what do we do on Monday?" I said out loud expecting no one to listen. In the silence, they did hear but no one answered. None of us seemed to know what we would do in our classes on Monday.

As our abbreviated potluck dinner ended, and as our colleagues were leaving, I said, "We don't know what to do for Crissy, or even if we can do anything. A student in trouble is always foremost in our minds. We are going to have to teach about President Nixon and Watergate on Monday. It is a national and international event that touches each of us and our nation. We also have to remember that the students in our class are human beings experiencing life in the increasingly difficult teen years."

"They sure are, and life for our teenage students is not getting any easier." Karla emphasized.

As we departed the potluck, I couldn't think of anything better to say than, "See you in school."

After everyone else had left except Megan, I said to Ana, "I will be back as soon as I can. Megan and I are going to see what we can do for Crissy and her mother."

Megan and I drove as fast as we dared to Crissy's house. When we arrived, we knocked on the door. Crissy's mother came to the door. "Oh, Ms. Straffa and Mr. Blenchard. I am so glad you came over. I have located Crissy. She is okay. She went to a friend's house. Her friend's mother talked Crissy into coming back home. She should be back shortly. Thanks to both of you for coming so quickly. I panicked and am still not over it yet. I will feel better when Crissy arrives. Can you stay until then?"

Megan looked at me as I nodded, "Yes, Mrs. Marlin, we can stay."

We stayed with Mrs. Marlin for about a half an hour. The door opened and Crissy came in. Both Crissy and her mother hugged as they shared tears. Mrs. Marlin held Crissy tight, not letting her go.

Megan and I knew it was time to leave. We were glad we could.

Chapter 21:
Crissy

"*S*he cut herself!"

"WHAT?" I exclaimed.

"She cut herself. Crissy, a junior in our high school, is in the hospital. Remember, the student who had been bullied that we talked about at one of our potlucks. She tried to slit her wrists. She tried to kill herself. God damn it." An emotional Megan tried to tell me what happened.

It was now Wednesday, May 8, 1974, eight months after our potluck discussion about teaching the "Saturday Night Massacre." On that Friday evening in October, 1973, Megan had reported that one of our students, Crissy, had been bullied.

Before Megan's news about Crissy cutting herself, we could not tell whether Crissy was getting better after being abused the previous year. As far as we could tell, nothing traumatic had happened to her recently. So we assumed that things had stabilized and maybe the bullying had stopped. Mrs. Marlin and Crissy appeared to have been doing alright, so I had put what happened to Crissy in the back of my mind, still there, but stored. Now, with the report from Megan, Crissy was again in the front of her teachers' minds.

After hearing what happened and my nerves had a chance to settle somewhat, I called Ana to see if we could host a potluck on Friday. Maybe if we got together we could comfort each other and see what we could do to help Crissy. Everyone could make it for our dinner except for Cheryl Wattsen who was accompanying her husband Cliff to a law-related weekend conference.

On Friday, May 10th, we exchanged greetings, got something to drink and eat. We moved into our circular seating arrangement so we could see and hear each other. On this night of concern for a student in trouble, we sat so close to each other that our knees touched. By now, we had dined together enough so collegial as well as personal friendships had developed.

As soon as we gathered, Megan reported what she knew after visiting the hospital on Thursday. "I could not see Crissy. Her mother was in with her when I got there. When her mother came out of Crissy's hospital room, she told me that Crissy failed at her attempts to kill herself. Her physical wounds were superficial and appeared to not be deep enough to do permanent damage. Her mother did not tell me this, but my guess is that the emotional scars may be a whole lot deeper."

At this point, Megan took a deep breath, sighed, and continued, "These teens we work with go through so much—all too frequently they ask, 'Who am I and does anyone care?' They are insecure about their popularity and about how they look. They fear failure academically. They worry about friends or the lack of them. And, now, we have this scourge of bullying. I realize bullying has been around for a long time, but it does seem to be getting worse. I don't know. I just don't know. What do the rest of you think? What do you think we ought to do for Crissy and for some of the other kids we have in class?"

At times like this when things get tough, Ken Lewiston is invariably helpful. He suggested with his usual calm demeanor, "Maybe in class if we give the students a chance to talk about issues facing teens today, maybe that could help."

Megan's angst oozed as her voice dripped with cynicism, "It's not in the school's curriculum, the school board and some of the parents do not want us talking about personally relevant matters. I know I am being negative but we get all kinds of complaints when we let kids open up."

Ken was normally unshakable. When it came to personal issues affecting students, his serenity evaporated. He tended to take things directly to heart. His sensitivity showed when students were troubled, and it was showing now. On this issue involving the welfare of a student he did not hold back. "People have been terrorizing people for a long time, and bullying, if that is what is happening here—if that is the problem here—it is harassment at best and terror at worst."

Karla Betts was still relatively new to our school, but we already realized that she was different and special. Karla had Crissy in one of her art classes. Karla proceeded to extoll Crissy's creativity. We all listened: "She sees things others don't. In her paintings, her use of color is dramatic. I should have talked and listened to her more. I missed the intensity of her pain. I feel awful. Crissy feels and senses the world around her. People have not always been kind to her. Crissy's art has been her way of connecting to her world. I hope some in that world have loved her back."

"I feel so helpless. I want to help in some way." Ana said.

"Me too," Derek Randallston added.

We were not sure if we felt better at the end of our discussion on this May evening, but we knew that talking with each other was comforting even though we still did not know what to do. Although we did not have any answers, we had shared our thoughts. For us, the sharing was a critical step in discovering possible solutions to this crisis or other latent problems. In any event, we all wanted to help Crissy. On this Friday potluck dinner, we felt that we had cleared our minds somewhat even if we did not have a plan to alleviate the pain Crissy was obviously experiencing.

As we were saying our goodbyes just before 11 P.M., which was later than we usually parted on our Friday evenings together, the phone rang. I picked it up not knowing who would call at this time of the night. My entire bodily expression must have shown its dread over hearing the news. Everyone stopped and looked at my ashen face. I hung up the phone and murmured, "Crissy is dead."

"What?" Megan Straffa said as she began to panic.

"Crissy walked out of the hospital. She must have gone down to the train station and stepped on the train tracks. She apparently waited for a train to come. It does not appear to have been an accident." I said.

Ken didn't usually get emotional in public, but as he spoke his eyes watered as they had when he talked about his students who have gone to Vietnam. "Damn it. These poor kids are just trying to grow up. We need to assist them in doing so. Damn it."

Heads down, hearts broken, Ana and I walked out of our home with our colleagues. We did not want to separate. In piercing silence, we hugged into the night's end. I remembered the time Megan and I saw Mrs. Marlin hold Crissy tightly not wanting to let go. We did not want to let go of each other on this night either. There seemed to be finality in releasing clenched arms.

The service for Crissy was held in the Community Church in town. The mostly Protestant church welcomed anyone who wanted to worship or just drop in, regardless of the religious persuasion or lack of one.

In life, Crissy must not have known that she had so many friends. The pews filled as people stood around the church. Those who could not get in to the service gathered quietly outside the church's front doors as a light rain fell. All were there to celebrate Crissy's life, a celebration she must have perceived little of in her own mind while alive. The cathedral embraced her as if she still lived. In her mourners' hearts—she did.

Unless she believed that nobody in the world cared, Crissy could not have imagined so many would stand outside to grieve her death. Umbrella-less throngs of people stood outside as grace drizzled.

Crissy's friend, Mary, delivered the eulogy as the church bathed the congregants. The eulogy stunned the somber crowd through teenage innocence. Only a soulmate could deliver words with telling resonance. Only a fellow student could understand. Only a friend could express the loss of beauty. Mary's words embraced the art contained in Crissy's short life.

Mary began in the strong, confident voice of someone who was certain of what she was saying. "Crissy, it is with great sadness that we come here today to call attention to your life and say goodbye. The beauty of your life was because you were different, beautifully different. You did not fight back against others when you were pushed because you didn't believe in pushing. You lived and let others live. You loved and let others love. We, your friends, family, and loved ones are going to miss you. Your creativity in Ms. K.'s class illustrated your unique gift for loveliness. We know that the heavens now have more imagination with you drawing pictures in the sky. Good-bye Crissy. No one will hurt you anymore. You are free to create forever."

Sobbing soaked the church. Mrs. Marlin could contain her loss no longer. Without Crissy there to hold, she reached for anyone she could find. She cried uncontrollably, without end. Her baby was gone.

Karla sat stone-faced. She felt to her core the emptiness and shock of losing a precious gift. Her heart ached, so did mine. I hold my heart tight. Karla releases hers. Male stoicism plagues me.

Crissy, who died when she was a junior in high school, was Karla's prized art student. To Karla, "student" is a sacred concept. In the church on that holy day, Karla's overt stillness gave way to muffled sobs. She felt the loss of a brightly shaded creative human being.

Karla loved her student. To teachers like Karla, each student is more than another person—but a sister, brother, son, daughter.

Quiet enveloped the church's whimper. The sanctuary's parishioners wept. One of its children had died.

Karla cried—Megan cried. I could not.

Chapter 22:
"Pressure"

"What could have helped a young person like Crissy? And, how can we help young people handle the pressure of growing up with all of the stresses currently affecting them?" I asked Ana.

"I don't know, Mark. I wish I did know. It tears my heart. The stresses in today's society are hard enough on adults—but for the kids—they aren't ready for it. The kids may never be. We have two children. I fear for them. They are growing up in this high pressure, high stakes world. I just don't know what to do. It seems as if everything is moving too fast. Joel and Suzie, like a lot of our students, are caught up in this whirlwind. Their lives are saturated with anxiety, tension, stress, and for some, bullying. I know I am stretching it a bit, but in a way all of this high pressure testing on our kids is a form of bullying. The constant testing at the very least is sometimes pushing the kids beyond their limits. I am sorry, but this high pressure schooling in the worse cases is bullying—bullying that is emotion-laden. And in some cases it is worse than physical. It is stripping the hearts out of our students and children. Of course, I realize that Crissy's bullying was of a different kind. But the pressure we all feel—the pressure to be smart, thin, beautiful, and so forth, is affecting us all. Some of the kids are just cracking—just cracking." Ana seldom became this heated about anything, but the pressure-cooker that was cooking in the schools was personal for Ana.

The schools have precious few counselors to handle the increasing number of young people like Crissy who could use some help in working through the problems teenagers encounter. Many of our students experience teenage angst. They often have no one to go to necessitating encountering life-affecting travails on their own. Often, they lack the tools to tackle adult-created problems.

In 1958, in response to the successful launching of the Soviet Union's Sputnik satellite in space on October 4, 1957, the United States Congress passed and President Dwight D. Eisenhower signed the National Defense Education Act. The act provided for, among other things, additional school counselors who would identify and counsel talented high school students who excelled in the school subjects related to science, technology, math and foreign languages. The theory was that identifying "talented" students would help in the nation's defense. Thus, the terminology in the act, "National Defense." Through this new legislation, the federal government thrust new obligations on the schools and students. The schools became the incubator for the nation's defense. This was a role for which the schools and its educators were ill-prepared.

As a result of the legislation, federal largess was aimed at improving teaching in science, math, and various languages— school subjects deemed to have implications for the nation's defense. Also included was financial support for improving the use of technology in the classroom. The Act provided funds so teachers could have the opportunity to develop technological skills. I went to a couple of summer institutes, received a stipend which helped to pay the bills, and picked up a couple of concepts and skills that helped me in my classroom. Many other teachers had similar experiences.

School counselors soon found that selecting talent was not their only necessary function. Assigned or not, school counselors increasingly became involved in counseling students, not just on academic issues, but on emotional issues as well. Counselors, using their expertise, extended their job descriptions to include working with students on a plethora of behavioral matters. Schools added concern for students' mental health as well as their intellectual development. Counselors increasingly assisted students with concerns out of school as well as in the schoolhouse—a difficult but vital task.

As the pressures of schooling have intensified, more and more students have been seeking emotional as well as academic help. Meanwhile, the government and school systems have increased the pressure placed on academics. They have signaled to students, some unready for the stresses, that the national defense and their schools' reputations depend on how well they do academically. The National Defense Education Act dropped the fate of the nation on students' sloping shoulders. The pressure planted on young, anxious psyches has affected their emotional development with sometimes devastating effects. School administrators rewarded the students who received high scores with a pizza party. Our principal, Ralph Giffin, provided pizza replete with double cheese. My disdain for the "pizza ceremonies" exuded at the "If you do this, I will give you that" deals the schools and our principal proffered for higher scores on tests.

Politicians and policy makers have pushed new curricula onto the schools and the students as politicos have perceived the demand for higher standards. Fairly or unfairly, the fate of the planet and defense of the nation settled on the students' hearts and minds—ready or not—necessary or not. The message that students occupied the first line of defense against "all enemies foreign and domestic" weighed heavily on any who were not prepared for the mammoth task of defending the nation in an era of increased uncertainty. The load crushed some students.

As a result of public policies, the job of preparing students for an uncertain and purportedly dangerous future landed on the schools. In the late 1950's, public officials blamed the nation's educational institutions for failing to prepare students for the contemporary challenges and those deemed ahead. School administrators have invariably passed the blame onto colleges of education and the teachers they educate. There has been an excess of "Not me" excuses, as the chiding and reproof passes from one office to another.

Thus, this urgency to save the world lay on students unequipped to take on such a heavy burden. Consequently, the demand grew for guidance counselors to save the "saviors" who were supposed to save the nation. School systems, thus, employed counselors to help students deal with the increased academic pressures. The academic pressures added to the stresses already inherent in growing up in the teen years.

Furthermore, under the watchfulness of national policy makers, there has developed an expanded reliance on high stakes testing. This has increased the burdens on schools. Some administrators and faculty as well as students buckled under government imposed unfunded mandates.

As I became more frustrated with the testing-craze and the resulting fervor, I said to Ana as we were sensing the pressures affecting Joel and Suzie as well as other children, "These pressures and parental aspirations for their children mean that getting into the 'right' college, after gaining admission into the right preparatory high school, after having gotten into the right elementary school, after having chosen the right kindergarten, after finding a place for your child in the right pre-school, and after purchasing the right audios and videos for your 'precocious' toddler have become the goals for some parents. This, in turn, has placed more pressure on a school system's administrators, counselors, teachers, students, and its public school board. And, Ana, on you and me as parents and on our kids. This frantic race is to somewhere; although, I don't know where the 'somewhere' is, and I don't think anyone knows where this is all going to end. This standards' fetish is leading people to become nervous wrecks and is not good for anyone. Especially not for kids."

Ana and I discussed these issues frequently. We now had two children who would be attending public school through high school. Both of us taught children who were subject to the increasingly high stakes' examinations and related demands. We felt the squeeze to our intellectual and emotional cores.

In one of our discussions, I asked, "Ana, do you see the high stakes pressures on the children in your elementary school?"

"Yes I do, Mark. The pressures are growing. It is in all of the elementary grades. In many ways, it is harming children. Kids can't just be kids anymore. They go home and do homework. Instead, they need to be playing outside enjoying the fall air and developing social skills with their friends."

"How do you see it manifesting itself in elementary school? The pressure I mean."

"I, and other teachers at my school, see young kids freaking out. You have told me about some of your high school students with test anxiety. We are seeing this in elementary school students too. We see more distraught students all the time. They are too young to handle the pressure. I don't know what the result is going to be but it doesn't look like it is going to be good."

"Yes, Ana, I agree that all of this pressure is overbearing for your students and mine. Some of my Bailey students are in a perpetual state of frenzy because they believe their entire future rests upon these high stakes standardized exams. In the school corridors, students are walking around like zombies. Tight faces, rigid bodies everywhere. I cringe when I think about it."

"Me too. Why are we educators doing this, Mark? I mean what is the point?"

"The bean counters are in charge. The policy makers don't know what to do, so they require tests whether it makes any sense or not. We know that all these tests do is measure how rich or poor the students are. The test makers don't know our students, indeed some of the test makers have never taught students and are assuming what teachers do in schools without really knowing. Moreover, the tests are created for someone else, not our students. Yet, the tests are used to measure our students like products and evaluate us as the producers. It is absurd."

Both Ana and I felt strongly about the issues resulting from the advent of the increased power of the testing industry. We wanted to hear what our colleagues thought. We scheduled a potluck dinner shortly after the school year started in September of 1975.

Chapter 23:
Jason

The testing industry affects what teachers do in our classrooms, and even though it influences what we do—testing is not even close to all we do. By our nature, we as teachers exude optimism. We walk into classrooms believing that what we do can and will change lives. We do so even when the odds are stacked against success for each student. Stubborn to the very end, we never give up. We do lose some but by no means all. We don't want to lose a single student, because when we do, it really, really hurts. Yet, on the other side of the hurt is teacher joy. Jason's story illustrates the point.

After Crissy's tragic death, Karla continued to be the teacher who cared for every student whether the student was in her class or not. If students needed an "in locus parentis," or even a "real" parent for a while, or a friend for a while, or a teacher for a while, or someone to talk with for a while, or just someone for a while or even a long while, they all knew where to find her.

Upon getting to know their teacher, Bailey High's students realized that Ms. K. cared to her core about each of them. What at first students thought of as "ditzy" was bottomless love for them and an endless belief in their ingenuity. Her modus operandi looked like chaos, but was the creative process at work. Gradually "Ms. Ditz" became a term of affection. Karla cradled the nickname.

I learned later that Karla had been abused as a child by a couple that took her now and then when her parents were traveling. Her parents were busy in the theater, so Karla did not "bother" them with the problems that came with the criminality. She kept it to herself, handled it herself, and lived with it. When she told me about the abuse, she said, "Those abusers hurt me. Even though the perpetrators are long gone, they still wound me every day, but they and their ghosts have never controlled me and never will."

Karla was one strong individual. You could try to get to her center but you could not. Her beat touched an artful drum. Her pulse gained strength as time went on. As one of her students who got to know her through as many classes with Karla as she could take, said, "You don't mess around with Ms. K. You can play with her, but you best not mess with her."

Karla's student, Jason, tested her patience; but he never wore her down. The perseverance Karla learned in her youth enabled her to stick with her student. The word "student" to Karla had that special meaning that teachers like her understand.

One night, Jason and a friend broke into a store. It wasn't the first time Jason had taken things that belonged to others, and once again he was caught with the goods in hand. Already with a record at sixteen years old and without enough bail money, he was put in jail to wait for trial. Jason's unkempt hair and shabby clothes led some people to treat him badly. While in the jail, he came into contact with some hardened criminals, as young as Jason. These youthful inmates found another young man who was to them a potential and attractive victim. To the predators, Jason was "easy pickins."

Karla was the only teacher to visit him in the jail. I wanted to go to see him, but I had not had him in class and was not sure if a visit would be appropriate or helpful. Besides, Karla said she would go to see him as often as possible which she did. After one of her visits, Karla returned to school in tears as she told me what Jason reported had happened to him. She said that two stronger inmates had been stalking him. Eventually, they attacked Jason and sexually abused him.

Karla reported, "They held him down making him perform oral sex on both of them as a sharp instrument was held against his neck. Then each had intercourse in his rectum. They wanted Jason to whimper and squeal but he would not. Jason admitted that the pain was excruciating, but that he did not cry or make any noise, especially the squeal they wanted him to make. To Jason, keeping that part of his dignity was important to him."

Karla said with tears in her eyes, "Jason told me that 'I cried, but not when they were on me. I cried later when I was alone.' Mark, I wish I had been with him when he cried."

Jason had grown up in the street. He had been in the criminal system early, and once in the pipeline it can be difficult to get out. The syndrome eventually ends in prison for too many young people, as it had for his attackers. Jason stole items from stores and got into fights. Karla continued, "Sure, Jason did some things he shouldn't have—but, Mark, he is, after all, just a kid. I am going to help him as much as I can." And, emblematic of Karla's character, she followed, "I would like to help those who attacked him too."

"Also, Mark, Jason has a legal guardian who has managed his affairs since he was ten years old. She has had trouble paying for court costs. Jason just can't extricate himself from the criminal system."

Jason, small for his age, had built himself up with weights and pushups. No one in high school wanted to fool with him because he had a fight to the finish ethic. His temper could flare at any time and his violent outbursts were spontaneous and unpredictable.

Fighting was Jason's claim to manliness. He had learned how to fight in the streets and fight he did—sometimes at the slightest challenge to his manhood or a perceived insult. He generally threw the first punch and was known for aiming at the testicles with a knee or if need be with a bite. His clenched teeth on an opponent's private parts was known to be disabling for the person on the receiving end. Jason was seemingly courageous but you could tell he was just another kid who was afraid deep inside. He was still a boy who wanted desperately to be a man so he could take care of himself.

Jason planned to stay in high school until he became the legal age to drop out. He did not know who his parents were. Over the years, Jason moved from relative to relative before gaining a guardian. His guardian took care of him as best she could but she had limited resources, so Jason had to move around. After a period of homelessness, he moved back in with his guardian. As a sophomore in Bailey High, he met Ms. K. and things began to change.

Karla was not very good at reading adults. "I don't do very well with adults." She said. "I am especially bad at intimate relationships. Some of them have turned out particularly badly. I would rather not give the details. But, Mark, you can probably imagine."

Yet, if Karla was not good at reading adults she could, on the other hand, scan a room full of teenagers and know them intuitively. Furthermore, she understood each student as an individual.

Karla zeroed in on Jason as soon as he entered her room on the first day of class in the fall of his sophomore year. Her empathy for Jason was instantaneous. Even Karla admitted that her understanding of Jason was so fast that it surprised her. She saw that there was a lot of him in her, and some of her in him.

In her tenth grade art class, Ms. K. recognized a young man who was afraid, lonely, lacking in confidence, and in need of an adult who did not judge him. Karla accepted Jason for who he was, without reservation. Because of her own past experiences, she knew what it was like to be rejected as a person and abused as if an object.

Karla knew where to draw the line. No romance with a student or even a hint of one. No visits to her house without calling first, and if alone not even then. Ms. K. remembered well what had happened to Derek Randallston for being in a parked car with a student without a chaperone.

And, no special favors for Jason that she wouldn't give all of her students. Jason had no one else so Ms. K. helped to fill the void. If he or another student needed a friend, she would be it.

After Jason's stint in jail, he needed to petition to get back into school. He had a criminal record now that needed to be expunged, preferably before his eighteenth birthday. Karla went to bat for him. He was readmitted to Bailey High when Karla said she would be responsible for him. If something went wrong, she was willing to lose her job for a student.

In addition to observing Jason's creativity in her class, Ms. K. saw her art student running on the school track one rainy day during lunch period. Jason could run, and he could run fast. He could not afford track shoes so he ran without them. Jason had never thought of running for the school track team. At Karla's urging, Jason tried out for the team. Still running without shoes, he made the team. He later said, "I run as if those two bastards who attacked me in jail are chasing me. I leave them in the dust." In high school track meets, his opponents couldn't catch him either.

Karla began going to Jason's track meets. He looked over to see if she was there. Unless she absolutely could not make it to Jason's races, she sat straight up smiling in the grandstands. Karla did not know about track events before attending them, but she learned fast. She soon punctuated her vocabulary with words like "sprint," "dash," "curbs," and "false starts." When she really wanted to strut her newly acquired knowledge, Karla would word-drop an "anchor leg" or two without taking her eyes off her stopwatch.

No one close to Jason could make it to his track meets. Track meets were scheduled immediately after school and many were away, especially the state meets. Jason's few relations in the area had to work and could not get out to cheer Jason on. Ms. K. could and did.

Karla found a way to attend the meets, even when they were held at other schools. If it mattered to Jason to have someone there, which it did, Karla would be there. When the state meets were held, she asked me, "Will you ride up with me, Mark?"

"Of course I will, Karla." They were some of the best rides I ever took.

With Karla's constant support and presence, Jason began to turn his life around. His grades in school improved. One day, he asked Karla, "Ms. K., do you think I could go to college and make it?"

It was an easy response for Karla, with a smile of joy when a student leaps, "Yes, Jason, I do."

"But I have a record."

"It is a juvenile record. You will be 18 when you go to college, and it should not have an impact and may in fact already be expunged from your record, or it will when you are of age. I will check on it. We won't let anything stop you, so please don't worry about it."

In his senior year, Jason's 100-yard dash times were good

enough to make a college team. His teammates valued him as a key member on the Bailey High relay team. Karla boasted that "Jason is particularly effective in passing the baton during relays."

Jason tried to get into colleges that were a reach for him. They had good track teams that he felt he could make. Each denied him admission. Karla recommended that he request an interview. She was sure that if admissions' personnel met Jason and experienced his desire for an education that he would have a chance to be admitted.

When the day approached for Jason to make visits to college admissions' offices, he needed someone to take him to the interviews. "Jason, I will take you to the interviews," Karla said.

On the morning of the college visits, Karla Betts was sitting in her car outside the apartment building Jason was staying in. Karla Betts and her colleague and friend, Megan Straffa, were ready to help a student go beyond where some others thought was possible.

As a teacher, Karla did not see limits, she saw possibilities. She knew where her student, Jason, could go. Karla was ready and willing to help him get there.

On that sunny collegiate visit day, Jason Burro, Ms. K. and Ms. M. drove toward hope.

Chapter 24:
"Eugenics"

egan Straffa, Ken Lewiston, Cheryl Wattsen, Charles Yates, Jake Spanner, Karla Betts, John Browne and Nancy Cash accepted the invitation to join Ana and me for our first group dinner of the new academic year. Zack Barber, who was new to the social studies faculty, also agreed to join the potluck group that had been meeting off and on for two years. Ana's friend and colleague from the elementary school faculty, Nancy Cash, responded to the invitation, "I would love to participate and discuss the issue of testing in elementary schools and beyond." The rest of the potluck group agreed that testing is an important topic for us to discuss.

After we fetched something to eat and drink on Friday evening, September 26, 1975, I opened the discussion by asking, "What are your views on the increased standardized testing we are facing in our schools from kindergarten through high school?"

As fast as she could say it, Megan said: "These high stakes tests are discriminatory. We should get rid of them."

"What do you mean?" Charles asked quickly.

"Well, first, a bunch of believers in eugenics and people like them created the SAT and similar high stakes tests like it."

"Who were they to do such a thing?" Charles said mockingly.

"Seriously, are you sure Megan or is this one of your propaganda pitches?"

"Come on Charles. This is the first potluck of the year. Are you going to start out on me again? Zack and Nancy have just joined the group. What will they think?" Megan said with a half-smile.

"Oh, okay, Megan, if you beg me to, then I will lay low for a while. However, you do seem at times to have a monopoly on intellectual rigidity."

"Nancy and Zack, close your ears for a moment because I don't want you to leave before we even really get started. Charles, screw you."

"Alright, already. Let's hold the barbs and sarcasm until our new members get used to this group's frankness," I said eliciting some laughter from the potluck veterans. Zack and Nancy looked puzzled at my request. It was clear they were enjoying the bantering, serious and not, and did not need a reason to explain the verbal skirmish between Megan and Charles. Zack and Nancy got it.

Ken, as he usually did, sought to focus on the issue and provide some information. "In an education course in college, I read about the origin of some of the standardized tests. We discussed in class about how the believers in eugenics tested, through standardized exams, their theoretical belief in white superiority. This occurred about the same time believers in race purity were making a move in Europe—in the 1920's. We all know what happened in the world as a result of the National Socialism movement. Well, in the United States at the time, there was a small but influential group of academics and politicians who believed that race was the determinant factor in intelligence."

"Yes, Ken, of course we have heard about racial theories, but I don't know a whole lot about it. Would you please give us more details?" Cheryl said. "And Ken, while you are at it, what was the philosophy behind the eugenics movement?"

"The eugenicists believed, and some people still do, that in order to have a good society the culture's leaders should purify the races by matching the pure white with the pure white, or as close to pure white as one can get. The philosophy dictates that people of color should not mix with the Nordic races. It is a race-based philosophical system with whites on top and people of color somewhere down the line. Insidious, I know, but that is what they believed."

"So, these guys who started the SAT and other standardized tests believed this crap?" Jake asked.

"Yes, that is what I am saying. The eugenicists, who believed in white superiority, did not have to manipulate the examination questions. They used testing to confirm their presuppositions about 'others.' It was a quintessential example of confirmation bias in action for the benefit of the few over the many. For example, many immigrants did not speak English and the exams were given to them in English. Obviously, the non-English speakers did not do very well. When so-called 'intelligence tests' were given to immigrants just arriving on Ellis Island in New York, the test-takers had not learned English yet. Guess how they did. It was not that they couldn't have done well if they had a chance to take it in their own language. It was more the unfairness of a system that stacked the deck against certain groups of people. Even if the test makers believed they were doing something good, they may unknowingly have enabled some people to win and other people to lose. Furthermore, some of the people of color did not do very well on the exams they were given either, in large part because they had an under-resourced education to begin with. Schools for minorities throughout the United States were segregated and under-funded. Separate was not equal. So, the tests proved nothing other than you could take the tests in a language foreign to you and not do well. Or, if you are under-educated you may not do well. Basically, the tests proved the bias of the test makers. As I said, a case of confirmation bias—meaning, we set things up so our bias is confirmed."

"Consequently, we based an entire educational system on a 'stacked deck' which just proved the bias of the test makers. Is that what you are saying Ken?" Megan asked.

"Yes, Megan, I believe that would be accurate to say. It is fair to say that is what I am saying. Basically, since the 1920's and the advent of scientific measurement, the system has been rigged. I started teaching in 1960. I have seen a lot of changes. And, if anything, the system has gotten worse. For example, another unfortunate phenomenon I have observed is that some administrators squeeze low performing students out of school. The 'low-performing' students are 'encouraged' to drop out. Then there are those who are on the 'bubble.' The kids on the bubble are right on or near the pass line. One or two points could be the difference between passing or failing the test. Hence, these students might not make the cut off score. Some school systems overly concerned with their ratings don't mind if the 'bubble kids' miss school on test days—if you know what I mean."

"Unfortunately, I think I get it. For those of us concerned about student dropouts, this is a case study of the unintended—or, maybe the intended consequences. Ken, with the increased emphasis on testing, are there other examples of testing bias?" Cheryl asked.

"Sure, but I can see John wants to say something."

"I can add to what Ken is saying." John joined in to the discussion. "If you have under-funded, over-crowded, ill-equipped schools, staffed by inexperienced teachers, then the result is under-educated kids who don't do well on standardized exams. Mark and I have discussed this before when we discussed my educational background.

"I would like to make another point. I think 'standards' is another one of those code words. I don't like being the one to point out the inherent bias in this whole testing culture, but I am willing to do so. White guys create the exams with cultural biases infused throughout the exams. Then they use the word 'standards,' assuming everyone knows what standards mean. And, besides, whose standards are we talking about? On what philosophic basis are these so-called standards created? We do not know. We never meet or have a chance to question the people who put these exams together. We don't get the opportunity to ask them what their philosophy of education is and what evidence they used to arrive at what they believe. Therefore, when people of color don't do well on standardized exams, then folks in power are able to say 'tough luck, you don't measure up to the standards.' But, who is to say that these are the standards students ought to meet? And, it just so happens that minorities generally don't meet what I would call artificial standards. These exams become an excuse for keeping some out of selective colleges, letting some in, and giving 'merit' scholarships to those who already have money. So-called standards are an excuse for keeping the power structure the way it is."

"I see the point John. But what would you put in its place? You have to have something to replace it don't you?" Cheryl asked.

"And, if you don't, you liberals should all stop whining." Charles said.

"Maybe you have to put something in the place of standardized exams and maybe you don't. There are other ways to measure whether someone ought to get into a certain school or job other than a standardized test. All these tests do is confirm what we already know—kids from low-income backgrounds generally do not do well on them. Besides, they do not have the money to hire coaches or expensive test coaching companies. The testing companies, the tutors, the testing industry and the tests themselves become, in effect, the gatekeepers. They regulate who gets in to the prestigious institutions, who stays out, and who gets society's advantages and goodies. If we gave low income kids a chance, they would excel—and, when we do give them a chance they do excel. We keep them out through this testing syndrome that we have instituted. We should give these students a chance and then watch them go. As far as admitting students to a given college, why not interview them. I realize it would take time and cost some money but it is a whole lot fairer than relying on standardized test scores. Karla, isn't Jason Burro going through the college interview process now? How is that working out?"

"John, I am glad you asked. Megan and I visited six selective institutions of higher learning with Jason. He has been admitted to three of them through personal interviews. He is in the process of deciding which to attend where he plans to try out for the track team."

"Bravo to Jason. Bravo!" Ana said as the dinner group broke into cheers and applause.

"That is, indeed, great what Jason has accomplished. And John, I am not a person of color but I completely agree with what you have said. Also, it is not just minority kids who are kept out through the testing system. Poor white kids don't have the advantages either. And, if you don't mind me adding, women get screwed too with these standardized exams written by and for a bunch of rich white guys. I must say I am not surprised with your analysis." Megan said.

"Megan, you seem to love that word 'screw.' Don't you?"

Charles said with a laugh.

"Yah, I do Charles. As long as it is not with you."

"Ouch. Don't worry Megan. You are safe with me. I wouldn't screw with you if you were...Oh, never mind."

"Yes. Never mind. Let's get back to the subject. This is a pretty important topic. And, it isn't only 'rich white guys' who run things. I would expand it to include wealthy folks in general, whether male or female." I said.

"Mark, I can accept that. I agree that it is not only male. It is a class thing." Megan said.

"This entire testing regime sounds like it favors primarily one group over a whole lot of other folks. How did we get into this fix? A lot of my art students are really smart and creative. Maybe that is why they don't do well on these exams that make everyone a standard. My kids think out of the box rather than fitting into the testing box. They out-think the test. Consequently, they don't get the advantages that high test scores bestow," Karla noted.

Ken added, "Karla, I think you are right on with what you just said. And, John has provided additional support that the standardized exams industry confirms what we already know. Children from wealthy families can buy an education for their kids. They pay for expensive tutoring to get their children ready for standardized exams, usually resulting in higher examination scores. The increased score gets them in the 'right' college. Then, as a result of the higher scores, the well-off students often receive merit awards, accompanied by financial support they often do not need. Furthermore, the higher scores get the wealthy family's progeny into the selective colleges that eventually lead to entry into prestigious law, medical or graduate schools. In the colleges and professional schools, these students meet others with advantages so they hire each other on Wall Street in New York or K Street in Washington,

D. C. Quite a little game isn't it?"

"Let me add that under-resourced schools are unable to provide their students with the tutors and the other tools that money can buy. If they were at the same starting gate as the kids with the advantages, the students in the less-privileged schools would also be able to succeed on the high stakes tests like the SAT. Assuming of course, that achieving a high score on the SAT has any merit at all. I, of course, do not believe it does." John said.

"It seems like a lot of kids are getting shafted. How do we break this cycle?" Megan asked.

Ken answered, "It won't be easy. The people who benefit from the system run the system. They have power and money which reinforce each other. Many of the elite send their own children to private schools, so as long as the public school kids don't compete for admission to selective colleges with the children of the elite, then the system works for them. Those who benefit from the system, of course, do not want to change the system they benefit from. In addition to tutoring, in the private schools the students learn the tricks of the testing trade which is exactly what it is—a trade."

"Yah, Ken, I get it. You learn the tricks—you get the treats." Zack injected.

"So the system works for them. The rich get richer. Is that how you see it?" Jake said.

"Yes, Jake, that is how I see it. It sure does make the rich richer. Unfortunately, this system of high stakes tests is also making the poor poorer. The testing gap feeds the income gap between rich and poor. In fact, the gap is widening. To me there is no doubt about it."

Jake's sarcasm spilled out, "This is all so unfair. Ken, do you mean that all the advantages our parents have bought us are useless if the system is made more equitable?"

Ana, seeing the facetiousness in Jake's comment, said, "I feel like crying, Jake. Your comment makes me think that I ought to laugh, but I ache for these kids. Many of them don't even have a chance in this system. I can't even chuckle."

"And, Ken, as you said, those who benefit from the present system are not about to change the system that rewards them. Is that right?" Karla said.

"Yep. That is the way it is as I see it." Ken responded.

"Shit." Megan said. "And, Ken, these people who run the system argue that the system is fair."

"Yes, they do. The mistake we make is that we believe it with them. We reinforce the system. When students in Bailey High get high scores, we make a big deal about it, have festive celebrations, eat lots of pizza, and publicize our alleged success. We feed the system that, in my judgment, harms our students as well as many other young people around the country; indeed, other countries in the world have bought into our system—test, test, test, and test again."

John added, "A good score on a standardized exam means nothing other than you did well on that exam. Some people assume that a good score on a standardized exam means that you are smart. In my judgment, it does not mean that you are smart or anything like that. It just means that you were good at that particular exam. Does it mean you are intelligent? No— I believe it does not. But as long as those who have money can hire tutors to help their kids get a higher score, the system will continue to exist as it has with some winners and a whole lot of losers. And, the winners are the ones who control the system. If low income kids became the winners, then those of us who taught them how to do well on the tests would be asked how we did it. According to the privileged few, teaching low income kids to do well on the tests is sometimes perceived as cheating because the system that rewards the elite is undermined. Of course, this is not cheating, but those who are supposed to win get angry and acrimonious when they don't, because they are supposed to win—always."

"And, John, as you said in an earlier discussion, a student who gets into the advanced classes gets even more advantages. They have smaller classes, the purported best teachers, and so forth. Thus, we provide the privileged kids with even more privilege. As Ken said in response to Karla's question, those with money have no incentive to change the educational system because they benefit from the way it presently is." I said.

"Yep. You've got it. Unfortunately, for the rest of us in this world, you have to know how the system works. We need to help everyone understand how the system works—not just the select few." John said.

"My goodness. I don't like this system because most of our students don't fit into the one size fits all dynasty. And, I mean dynasty."

"Hey Mark. You usually don't use those kinds of words like 'dynasty.' Sounds like you might become a liberal after all." Megan said eliciting laughter.

"And, John, if I believe what I am hearing, as you said, those who control the system will argue that the system is fair."

"Yes, Mark, you have got it. Pretty good for a white man." Laughter erupted in the group as John cracked a smile.

"John, Ken, or anyone else who wants to answer this. Will the SAT ever go away? What do you think? I am concerned because this testing mania is reaching deep into the elementary schools." Nancy said.

"As long as parents can pay for tutoring and those who pay to play –win—things are not likely to change." Ken said.

"But, they say tutoring doesn't make a difference." Zack said.

"Oh, yah, tell that to the test preparation companies who intimate through their advertising that test-coaching makes a difference. Also, if parents really believe it does not make a difference then ask them why they are spending their hard earned inherited money to pay for tutoring. They know it works. Only the people who run the testing companies and the SAT exams want us to believe it does not matter. Their argument runs at cross purposes and does not hold up. The testing companies charge a lot of money for the tutoring, so they can't say it doesn't work even if it didn't which, of course, it does. School systems buy the oxymoronic argument both ways. Tutoring does work—they know it does and we know it does. Yet, to ward off criticism of this special benefit for rich kids they argue it doesn't matter. Oh, yes it does. Balderdash." Ken said.

"Does anyone know what SAT stands for? Huh, can anyone tell me?" Jake asked.

"I have not been able to find out. Is the A for achievement? Is the A for aptitude? Or, is it the Scholastic A. Test? Or, is it simply the SAT so you can pencil in the blank as to what it means in one of their patented multiple guess questions?" Zack said with a laugh.

"So, in an essential way, many of our students do not have a real chance, or equality of opportunity. If everyone had the same advantages, then the same people wouldn't keep winning all of the time." Megan said.

"I think that is correct. Our Bailey High students are as smart as anyone else. With similar advantages, our kids would do as well in school and in life. Of course, some of them do fine anyway without the advantages, but some do not do well because they do not have an equal start. If our students began the race from the same starting line with the privileged kids, then merit really would win out. We are fooling ourselves to think merit is winning now. We don't know who writes the tests, whether they have been teachers or not, what their philosophy is, or what their idea of a best answer is."

"So, Ken, if everyone were given an equal opportunity in the race to the top of the pecking chain, and everyone began at the same starting post, then we might get different outcomes. Is that what you are saying?" Cheryl asked with a pained expression.

"Yes. I think that summarizes it for me anyway."

"Then, if everyone had a really fair chance at doing well on the tests the children from wealthy families would not be getting all the goodies or even more than their share of goodies." Cheryl said.

"That would be revolutionary." Zack said.

"Once again you all are preaching a sort of class warfare. Are you sure that is what you really want to do. Frankly, I have heard enough of this bullshit."

"Charles, watch your language." Megan said as we all reveled in the irony.

"You, Megan, toilet mouth herself, telling anyone else to watch their language. That is a quintessential jest, assuming you understand the big word."

"Charles, I know you don't understand subtleties, but I was being wry. Do you want me to define the word 'wry' for you—or do you only understand the big words. You bastard. No, calling you a bastard is a slur on bastards. You are just a plain ole asshole."

"Come on everyone. We don't want to go overboard. Charles, you were just about to say something else."

"Yes, Mark, I do have something else to add. Once again everyone, I have heard enough to conclude that you all sound like a bunch of socialists. Why not let the capitalistic system work? It has worked for us so far in our history. If people work hard and earn money, then they will be able to have a better future and provide for a better future for their children. What's wrong with that, Megan?"

"No Charles, you have it wrong again. We are not for an equal outcome. We are for an equal chance for everyone. As has been quoted many times 'nothing is more un-equal than the equal treatment of un-equals.' So, if you start at the same place but some already have advantages then it is not really a fair contest—it is not equality of opportunity—you basically have a predetermined winner. That is not fair at all. I thought you were an equal opportunity type guy. All I am asking is that everyone should start from the same starting line without anyone having a special advantage. To use a sports analogy, which you as a guy should understand—we need a neutral referee. Then if you have different outcomes, then I am okay with that. But, let's at least start from the same place. No special advantages for anyone. Then merit would truly win out."

"Megan, I am for fairness. We have freedom in this country. All you have to do is work hard. What could be a fairer way of doing things?" Charles asked.

"Well, you would have to provide more for those who have less." Karla said.

"Like I said, socialism. You all are getting too close to that ideology. I wouldn't go there if I were you. The American people are not for socialism."

"Charles, you don't have anything to worry about. Fat chance governing bodies would make things more equal. The legislators either are wealthy themselves, or they represent the plutocracy. We aren't even close to becoming a socialistic country." Jake said.

"Charles, I usually don't have much to say in these kinds of arguments, but wealthy families spend gobs of money on their kids. We could use some of that money to make things fairer. For example, we could have an Individual Educational Plan for each student. An I.E.P." Ana said.

"Ana, that would cost way too much in taxpayer money to provide an I.E.P. for every single student. Our country cannot afford that." Charles said.

"In general, I am in sympathy with your argument Ana and some of the rest of you. But an I. E. P. would cost too much for the taxpayers. I think I am with Charles on the expense part. I agree the present system is not fair, but an Individual Educational Plan for every child is not realistic and would cost too much. The taxpayers would not go for it. In fact, I would not go for it." Cheryl said.

"Yes, Cheryl, I am glad someone agrees with me on something. We already pay too much in taxes."

"Sure. It would be costly, but I don't think it is too much to ask in order to make things fairer for more students. It would give more kids a fighting chance." Ana said.

"Yes. I agree with Ana. We need to do something to provide everyone with an equal chance. The pressure is growing on our little ones in the elementary schools. I look forward to some solutions in our future discussions. I am really concerned for my elementary school students, really concerned." Nancy said.

"It is now 11:15. Time to call it a night. Ana and I are going to bring Joel and Suzie to play dates and other activities in the morning. Just to summarize, though, I think that our high stakes testing discussion has shed some light on what is and maybe on what could be if we equalized things. On Monday, though, we will have to deal with reality. We have to get our students ready for upcoming standardized exams. Some kids will win and some will lose. Is this the only alternative we have? I don't know. But, clearly, we should take on this topic again."

"Oh, Mark, you act like a teacher even with fellow faculty in our potluck dinners. You summarize for us." Megan said with a sly smile. "However, to be serious for a moment as we are ending up, your real world comments at the end of our dinners are sometimes so depressing."

"I don't see Mark's comments as depressing at all. I think they are realistic. Life is not fair, guys. Life is just not fair. Is it Mark?" Charles said.

"Okay, Charles, tonight you have had the last word. I will see you all in school on Monday. I am sure we will discuss this issue again in a future potluck. Good night and be safe."

Chapter 25:
"Nam"

"Why did we get into Vietnam in the first place, Mr. M.?" The war ended over a year earlier, but my students still asked this question frequently.

In April of 1975, President Gerald Ford made the announcement ordering the last American troops out of South Vietnam. This was the second major public decision Ford made after he became president in August of 1974. The first announcement riveting the country's attention was when Ford pardoned his predecessor, Richard M. Nixon, on September 8, 1974.

President Ford was the first president who had not been elected vice president and then ascended to the presidency. Even though the electorate had not voted him into either office, Ford became president of the United States. It is difficult to lead a republic that you have not been elected to lead.

The conflict in Vietnam and the involvement of the United States in the war was a heart-wrenching period for the nation. Even though the war had ended, the chasm widened between those who were for the Vietnam conflict and those who were against. The pro-war and anti-war partisans continued to fiercely assail each other through hate-filled acrimony, mostly with words but not always. Police with swinging batons had removed trespassing demonstrators from public places. Insults had greeted veterans returning from Vietnam. Both sides spit out ugly vitriol. Opponents of the war asked, "Who was to blame for what happened in Vietnam?"

Our Friday night potluck dinner discussion on May 16, 1976, still burned with this issue. We had planned to start this Friday session with personal and school discussions. That did not happen on this evening because the events spawned by the war in Vietnam were so important and relevant to each of us that we could not elude them, nor did we want to. The residue of the war resided deep in the private and public consciousness of Americans.

Important national and international issues dominated the years leading to the national elections of 1976. A number of public controversies drew our attention. The conflict in Vietnam triggered intellectual and emotional firefights. We knew we had to teach about the conflict and do so fairly—not an easy task for an event jammed with controversy.

Even though it was clear prior to our gathering that Vietnam would be our focus, I started the potluck as usual asking if there were any personal, student, teaching or school issues. Everyone passed so I quickly moved into the issue of the evening, "Now that American troops have been out of Vietnam for more than a year, and we have had time to reflect, should we ever have been there in the first place?"

Charles responded quickly, "Of course we should have gone in with military force. It was the right thing to do."

"Why do you believe that Charles?" Ken asked.

"Obviously, the goal was to stop Communism and its aggression from spreading. We were trying to prevent the domino effect from happening—the idea that once the Communists take over in one country then they try to take over neighboring countries leading to countries falling like dominos to Communist control."

"But, we had no business interfering in a civil war in another country, like Vietnam. Did we?" Ken responded.

"Yes, we did, to protect capitalism and our way of life. It was the right thing for our country to do."

"What do you mean our way of life?" Megan interrupted. She then asked rhetorically, "You mean we need to protect our way of exploiting women and keeping minorities down? Is that as you say, 'the right thing to do?'"

"Oh, come on Megan—your comment is ridiculous."

"No it isn't Charles, and don't call my comments ridiculous. Okay."

Voices rose. I tried to calm things down. "I realize this is a difficult issue. Can you two find common ground?"

"No, I cannot agree with anything Charles says about the war. It was unnecessary. Look at all the Americans who were killed and wounded, and then there is the psychological damage that war leaves in a society. We should not have been in Vietnam in the first place."

Zack joined in, "Vietnam was an unnecessary conflict. Our national security was not threatened. I am quite sure of that. In my judgment, it was a waste of our national treasures."

"Sorry, Zack. Our national security was threatened and still is in various places in the world." Charles retorted.

"Oh, come on Charles. You sound like a war-monger."

"Damn it Megan. Here you go again. Calling me names."

"Well, you call me names too. Charlie."

In an effort to cool things down, I tried to change the subject, "Should President Ford have pardoned Nixon?"

Megan came back, "That is cute Mark, trying to change the subject, but actually it is the same subject. The Vietnam War and Watergate are linked. Nixon was involved in both. That jerk should have been impeached, not pardoned."

"Watch your language Megan, he was president and deserves our respect—calling a former president a 'jerk' is dissing the office. You should not do that." Charles continued. "Nixon was just trying to protect the country in both cases."

After a pause as Megan steamed, Charles added, "And, besides, Ford was trying to move the country along. The pardon was the right decision. It saved the country from more emotional and constitutional conflict at a time we did not need either."

"But, don't we need to know what happened in Vietnam? It has affected a lot of Americans. Truth matters doesn't it?" Cheryl asked.

"Sure we do need to know what occurred, Cheryl, but we need to know the full history in context. We need to know that Nixon was trying to defend the United States. And, it has worked so far. In the year or so, since we left Vietnam, other nations in Southeast Asia have not fallen like dominoes. So, mission accomplished."

"Yah, Charles, your version of the truth. You don't give that version in class, do you?" Megan seethed.

"Sure I do. I provide the students with the truth. Not propaganda or media spin like some other teachers I know. Are you a spinner in class Megan?"

"Oh, fuck you Charles. You are really pushing my buttons now. You have a bunch of opinions about Vietnam and other things. You ought to keep those to yourself and out of the classroom." Megan flashed a glance at Charles as the argument heated.

"Oh, I see Megan. Your opinions are alright in class, but mine are not. Besides, the truth about Vietnam is that the United States was trying to contain communism and the effort has been worth it."

"Charles, I have facts to back up what I say in class. My

opinions are based on fact. Yours aren't."

Charles' voice grew louder as he responded, "Wow. It is getting clearer to me Megan, your opinions are factual and mine are not? You, my dear Megan, are delusional."

"Don't call me dear, and I am not delusional. Charles, you are being a real prick."

"Huh. Getting defensive are you? Sorry if I offended you by providing you with the truth—Dear!"

" Are you trying to really piss me off? If you have been trying, Charlie, you have succeeded."

"Oh, Megan, don't be such a drama queen."

"Damn it! Stop calling me a drama queen. You sexist bastard."

"Stop calling me a bastard you b..."

"Yah, Charles, you better not say it."

"Alright. Alright. Let's get back to the issue. And, please reduce the personal affronts. That kind of language doesn't get us anywhere." I said.

"All those lives, Charles. All those lives. Was it worth it? I don't think so but apparently you think so. Charles, you really are such an asshole."

"Again, watch your language. Didn't Mark ask us to be more civil to each other? And, Megan, don't you think you need to grow up?"

"Please Charles and Megan, let's get back to the issue of how we should teach about Vietnam and its aftermath. I realize this is a hot topic, but we are teachers, so maybe we can better control the rhetoric." I said hoping to cool the personal hyperbole, at least momentarily.

On we went, late into the night. The raw rhetoric did not produce any conclusions, but we did put our beliefs and feelings out in the open so they could be examined and critiqued. The caustic interchange between Megan and Charles illustrated the rigid lines that had been drawn in the country. Vietnam and its consequences continued to dwell deep in our personal and national consciousness.

We agreed by the end of the evening to try to understand each other and our respective points of view. We could not decide which version of the truth was, indeed, the truth. We decided that we should present in our classes as many versions that had evidentiary support as we could discover. Then we would let the students make up their own minds. The country was simultaneously involved in the same wrenching post-war debate.

Because the emotions were so fresh from the evening's altercation, Charles and Megan did not shake hands goodbye. To their credit, the two teachers agreed to consider team teaching when their classes discussed the controversy. If they did so, their students would have the opportunity to contemplate different perspectives. The students would be voters soon and have to decide. They would have a chance to make better decisions if they considered multiple versions of what was happening in their world.

We, as teachers, all agreed that what the students believed was less important than how they arrived at their conclusions. We hoped to generate a careful examination of all sides through critically thinking about the facts and the possible options for future actions. Through this active evaluation of the evidence, the theory held that the students could arrive at warranted conclusions. As educators, this is what we hoped for and were after. The United States, including the future citizens in our classes, would have to decide what to do next.

Chapter 26:
Mrs. Bennett

*D*iscussions about the Vietnam War persisted as the new school year got under way in September, and they continued into October of 1976. After another week of intense class discussions about Vietnam and its residual effects, and the actions of presidents Nixon and Ford, I was ready for a break. The pressure, anguish, and the joy of teaching make time with family, friends, or an occasional night out on weekends look good. I usually had preparation for class, grading, or calls to make on Saturdays and Sundays, but Friday nights were usually my one night off.

I looked forward to the potluck dinners, but because we were all busy with our professional and personal lives the Friday night potlucks were not as frequent as I would have liked. So, after a particularly deep and divided series of personal interchanges in my classes about the Vietnam conflict I was ready for some relaxation on this particular Friday. I hoped to do something different to get my mind off of things. I didn't want to think beyond what I was going to have to eat.

Once I started teaching, I enjoyed and learned from attending social events in the Gorham community. It gave me a chance to get to know the parents of some of my students and members of the community at large. Therefore, when I was invited to a party at Mr. and Mrs. Dawson's home, I considered going. I had a personal policy that I would not attend an event where there was alcohol when a student attending Bailey High was present. Angela Dawson was still a student in Bailey, but her father said that during the party she would be at a movie theatre with friends, so there was no reason that I should not attend. Ana had a playdate planned for Joel and Suzie at a friend's house, so she said I should go alone.

I arrived at the Dawson's home fashionably late because I did not want to appear too anxious although I was. Their home is considered to be in the best part of town close to where Charles lives. There is a pool in the backyard but the fall air made it too cool for a dip. I was comfortable dressed in a long sleeve shirt with a sport coat. I had a tie in my coat pocket in case I needed it to fit in. I wore a tie when teaching, but the invitation to the party recommended "country club casual" as the dress code. I kept the tie out of sight but it was there if I needed it to fit in to a more formally dressed crowd. I wanted to just melt in without being noticed.

As I entered the home, Mr. and Mrs. Dawson graciously welcomed me as if I were a special guest. As others came in, the Dawson's made the new arrivals appear special too. It must be the way to do it in this part of the town.

The Dawson's home struck me as huge. My family could fit in one quarter of the house. The furnishings looked like they had been imported from Asia. I made my way into the back yard. The crisp autumn day's lengthening shadows stretched splendidly as dusk began setting in. I love the fall when the sun dances through flicking leaves.

I was hungry so I quickly sampled some hor d'oeuves. While standing around making small talk with other guests I hardly knew, I drank a couple of beers which was my limit. I planned to find the buffet table, have dinner, have some coffee and then drive home.

While finishing dinner and a piece of carrot cake, I sat alone at a table near the pool when Mrs. Harriet Bennett approached me. Her daughter, Barbara, was in my class. Mrs. Bennett looked like she wanted to talk. I had heard from Cheryl Wattsen, who also had Barbara in class, that Harriet Bennett had divorced recently, but still insisted on using the Mrs.

Harriet Bennett, probably in her mid-forties, looked like she was in her early thirties. She obviously worked out and must have spent a small fortune on her clothes. I did not find her attractive, although most people probably would.

Mrs. Bennett asked if she could join me. I was beginning to feel self-conscious sitting by myself, so I was glad to have the company.

"How are you doing Mr. M., or may I just call you Mark?" Mrs. Bennett didn't seem to care particularly but she asked anyway.

I uttered a matter of fact, "I am fine, thanks for asking, and please do call me Mark."

"Mark, there is something I would like to talk to you about. Could we take a walk?"

I had no idea what it could be about but Mrs. Bennett was a parent of a student so I politely, albeit slowly and warily, said, "Sure," not knowing what was going to happen next but becoming more guarded. Indeed, Mrs. Bennett was a parent of a student in one of my classes. I hoped she did not want something I could not or would be unwilling to do. My "caution ahead" antenna sprung.

The Dawson's home had a public park located just outside the fence in the back yard, so we strolled down the closest path. I couldn't imagine what Mrs. Bennett wanted to talk to me about.

Shortly after we started strolling, Mrs. Bennett did have

something important to discuss on her agenda. "My daughter Barbara is getting a C in your class. In order to get into a good college and obtain financial aid, which we will need because of the situation with my husband, she will need to get an A. I am sure you understand."

I stopped walking. An uncomfortable silence took over as the crackling on the gravel path ceased. I wanted to make sure I was hearing correctly what she was saying to me. "Mrs. Bennett, could you please say that again?"

"Let me make it perfectly clear, Mr. M. I want Barbara to get an A in your class and am willing to do what is necessary to make sure it happens." As she was telling me what she wanted, she moved close enough to me so the back of her hand made contact with my penis. It began to thicken. I am a little slow about such things now and then, but I was getting this message. I got that pit in my stomach as I recalled what had happened to Derek Randallston for being in a car with a student. Here I was with the mother of a student who wanted me to give an A to her daughter, and she was pressing against my private parts to make it happen.

I turned away from Mrs. Bennett. I started thinking about anything but what had just happened and my involuntary response to her hand. The thoughts of anyone seeing my bulging pants led to blood leaving my body and the thickness swiftly evaporating. As I felt my blood surge back and forth, I turned back facing Mrs. Bennett.

Simultaneously surprised, embarrassed and alarmed at what had happened, I stood before her fully blushed while she baited the question, "So, what do you say Mr. M.? There could be more of that, much more. I am sure you know what I mean."

I didn't have to even think about it as I said, "Mrs. Bennett, no deal."

As I turned to return to the party, she cautioned, "Don't say anything to anyone about this. They won't believe you. Your belly falls over your belt buckle and no one would believe that a woman like me would be interested in a guy like you. In fact, I would turn it around and tell people that you are the one who touched me and propositioned me. You would be brought up on sexual assault charges. How much money do you have to defend yourself in court? And, oh, just a thought, you would look good in the orange jumpsuits they make you wear in prison. If all this is not enough for you Mr. Blenchard, I will just tell you that Mitchell Appletone, your boss, is a good friend of mine. And, I mean a good friend if you know what I am saying."

"Mrs. Bennett, I am not sure I know what you mean by a good friend of yours?"

"Oh Mark, you are so clueless about the ways of the world."

"I have to go now, Mrs. Bennett."

"Is that all you have to say?"

"I guess so," I said as I spilled words. "Yes. I don't know what else to say. I have heard enough. Enough so that I do not feel very well right now."

"Well, I guess this concludes our little interaction. I trust you will do the politic thing. Just give me a call when you are ready to talk and we could get things going. I am sure I don't have to spell it out for you. In the meantime, Mr. M., good-bye and good luck."

Mrs. Bennett turned around with a satisfied smile on her face as she walked back toward the party ahead of me. I followed meekly, in no hurry to get back to the Dawson's home. I was not sure what to say or do. I left the Dawson's without saying goodbye to anyone. The pit sat ensconced in acid in the bottom of my stomach. I knew I had better get home before the pit disgorged in a bevy of vomit.

Mrs. Bennett's daughter, Barbara, earned a C in the history course she enrolled in with me as her teacher. And, whether it was politic or not, on the Bailey T. S. Memorial High School's official student issued report card, Mrs. Bennett and Barbara eventually eagle-eyed the C Barbara received for her efforts in the United States history class she took.

I never said anything to anyone about the walk in the park with Mrs. Bennett. I didn't even tell Ana. I knew Mrs. Bennett would attend Barbara's graduation. On that joyous night, I stayed away from anywhere I thought she might be. I made sure our eyes did not swap glances. I never called.

Chapter 27:
Maria and Ricky

"*I* am going to have a baby." Karla reported her student Maria telling her. "Then I will have someone who loves me and I will have someone to love."

"What? What did Maria say to you?" I said not believing what I was hearing.

"Maria, a seventeen-year-old junior in my third period art class, wanted to get pregnant and she was going to find a boy or a man who would fulfill her wish, not marry her, but give her someone to love. Maria told me, 'Anything is better than the loneliness I feel.' Maria apparently just couldn't stand being in her perceived perpetual state of being loveless. She wanted someone to love so she would not be lonely anymore. Maria was going to get her baby and get it she would. She was determined to do what was necessary to make it happen. And—she did."

Karla's efforts to talk Maria out of having a baby proved fruitless. Maria found a boy, Ricky Brezos, who was as desperate as she was for a few minutes of intimacy. Karla said, "Ricky, who is in Bailey High but I have not had him in class, must have needed love as much as Maria did. Or, as they saw it, they would have something resembling love. It would at least be something. Desperation can lead you into strange places."

Karla continued, "Maria asked Ricky if he would do it. He said he would. They arranged to meet and have intercourse. Maria's insecurity about her overweight body led her to try to hide who she was, although just about everyone thought she was beautiful throughout. She asked Ricky if he would do it in a dark room. That way he could not see her. Ricky apparently had no problem with what Maria looked like. However, he agreed to her request. They got it on without any physical light. Maria got pregnant after one time. She had apparently timed it so she would get pregnant after doing it just once with Ricky. It worked."

Personal loneliness among young people and their desire to have someone love them are more widespread than I could have imagined prior to becoming a teacher.

Some of the pregnancies are planned. Maria wanted to get pregnant and she did. The issue of teen pregnancy is complex. As with Maria and Ricky, teenage pregnancies aren't necessarily unplanned. Indeed, some of them may be better understood as part of a plan.

At the outset, the relationship between Ricky and Maria was not at all about sex—it was more about love—not their love, although there may have been some of that; but about love of, by and for somebody, almost anybody. In the case of this pregnancy, it was a baby born of a teenage mother. The baby resulting from the sex would be the love object who would return the love. As Maria reasoned it, then, "At least someone loves me."

Even though the baby love in this case may have resulted from dependency, to Maria it was love nonetheless—a love to fill a void in her life. Ricky wasn't necessary, but the baby was.

Maria was the daughter of a single parent. She lived with her father who took care of her the best he could. The three jobs he had as a custodian took him away from home seven days a week including holidays. Some parents work two or three jobs to send their children to private school. Maria's father worked multiple jobs in order to clothe, feed, and pay the rent for an apartment for him and his daughter. Her mother died during childbirth—Maria's birth.

Karla said, "Maria told me she was alone most of the week except when her father was home to sleep. The loneliness had become too much for her—she wanted someone to be with— hence, the baby. Maria concluded the husband was not necessary but the child was. All Maria wanted from Ricky was an instrument with active semen in it. Any hugs and kisses were extra but not required. It was all about the baby."

Some school systems have policies against pregnant students staying in school. A "No pregnancy in school" policy governed our school district. A pregnant Maria could not stay in our classes. She could not even come in the building. Presumably, she would "infect" her classmates or maybe transmit ideas to others. What disease, physical or mental, Maria would spread and how she would spread it was a mystery to me. Ricky could stay in school as long as he did not bring an expectant Maria in the building with him. The policy shocked Karla.

Karla wanted to test and change the policy directive. She believed that Maria should be able to continue her education and was ready to battle for her right to do so. With her iron-clad determination on behalf of a student, Karla declared to me, "Maria deserves and needs an education. I really don't see why she can't have one. I am going to do what I can to see that she gets a chance to get educated."

Karla was furious when Maria was told she had to leave school. "Why, Mark, why?"

I asked Karla to lead our next Friday potluck on Friday,

December 19, 1976. I thought that the last "Why" question she asked me would get the group going. The essence of the issue was "Why does Maria have to leave school?" Karla agreed to lead with that question phrased her way.

In December of 1976, Zackeri Barber returned to the potluck dinner group after having replaced Derek Randallston in the fall of 1975. In addition, Ana's friend, Nancy Cash, a second grade teacher in Gorham Center Elementary, again joined our group. Ken Lewiston, Karla Betts, Megan Straffa, Cheryl Wattsen, Charles Yates, Jake Spanner, and John Browne also attended. Ana and I continued to host the session.

After we got settled, Karla asked the group, "Why should someone like Maria, who needs and wants an education, have to leave school because she is pregnant?"

Charles answered briskly, "Because it is the rule. Pretty simple."

Karla, who seldom raised her voice, couldn't hold back, "Damn it, Charles, when people are involved it isn't that simple."

"Yes, Charles. I agree with Karla. You are wrong on this." Ana said.

Ana characteristically said little during our potlucks, but she could not stay out of this one. The issue resonated with Ana, "Maria should be able to get an education and should not have to go to night school to get it."

"We don't make the rules," Charles countered. "If you want to make the rules, then run for the school board."

"That's not a bad idea. If she did run for the school board, Ana would at the very least understand what it is like to have kids. Ana has children—you, Charles, don't. A lot of people on school boards don't have offspring either. They have no clue what parents and children go through when kids face the pressures of schooling. Charles, some of the school board

216

candidates who understand these kids don't get elected, whereas some of those who don't know an iota about kids do get elected because they think it will look good on their political resume. In addition, now that I am on a roll, I believe that school boards are all about conserving the community's values, not changing things. School boards go about making kids like the generation before them. The curriculum does not prepare students for the future but for the past. School boards are the last place we can look for change agents." Megan said with a sigh signaling hopeless abandon.

"Oh, Megan, here you go again with your cynicism. What makes you think that you know better?"

"Because, Charles, I teach kids day in and day out. I am with them all the time. I hear and feel their hopes and aspirations, and I hear about their frustrations."

"I agree with Charles." Cheryl said, "I believe Maria ought to be able to get an education, but not with regular students. It would be so distracting. We already have enough distractions. Don't we?"

By now, Karla was as seething as she ever gets, "This is a young woman's life and her child's life we are talking about."

"Well she should have thought about that before." Charles countered.

"Charles, you really have the ability to irritate me with your self-righteousness and pompous pontifications." Megan had already said her piece and tried to stay out of further debate but could not help herself.

"Why are you girls, except Cheryl, ganging up on me?"

"Oh, poor Charlie. 'The girls are ganging up on me.' First, we are not girls. Second, you deserve it you chauvinistic asshole." Megan bit back.

"Okay, okay. Can we please calm down? Once again we are discussing an issue that hits close to home. But, in order to discuss it we have to try to control our passions." I said.

"Why, Mark, are you trying to stop a good discussion? We were just getting going. You censor you." Cheryl said as she and the others chuckled.

"Okay. Okay. Say whatever you want. Just don't take it personally. Remember. We have to work together next week." My comments elicited an unintended laugh as some of the tension broke.

"Who said we were taking it personally. Besides, I don't mind being called an asshole. I believe in free speech. Even when Megan is wrong, which is most of the time, she has the right to be wrong. She is pretty consistent in missing the point but it is her right. If being wrong meant that one could not speak, then Megan would be quiet most of the time. Which might be welcome, at least by me." Charles was smiling as he applied a final needle. Megan didn't smile, but she sent back a mild growl indicating that she was okay even in her disagreement with what was being said.

By now, Zack and Nancy were active members of our group. I still wondered how these new group members perceived our discussions, especially when things got loud as they did when Megan and Charles clashed. "Zack, what do you think about these potluck dinner discussions?"

"They are refreshing." Zack had not said much to his colleagues since he had joined the faculty. He knew he could be caustic which tended to offend others. It was obvious that he was holding his sentiments close until he got more comfortable with the group. We wanted to hear from this new member of our potluck. We listened carefully to what he had to say.

"I don't have a problem with the honesty. I welcome it. I haven't said much yet, but I will in the future once I get used to the flow of this group. I am getting more and more comfortable with all of you here and in Bailey High. I have seldom experienced anything like this. Bring it on. As far as I am concerned, the more free speech the better. I welcome the directness. I just have to get used to it, so I will be comfortable enough to put my two cents in. Most people I encounter smile as they cut your throat, so to speak. In this group, you just dissect. The open discussions are unusual and refreshing. I believe I am in for the long haul just as long as we don't take it home with us and into the school."

"How about you Nancy?" I asked.

"I love Ana, and I love this. I am glad I joined this group. Go for it."

"So, you will keep coming back?"

"Can't wait. I, like Zack, find the verbal fireworks provocative in a good way. Just call me a potlucker." Nancy said.

The group chuckled as the terminology "potlucker" settled in.

We did not have any solution to the dilemma Maria's situation presented, but we had aired our views and we had two new "initiated" group members who were willing to stay with us as we confronted personal and professional concerns in school and out. We all looked forward to another candid exchange of views during our next potluck.

To our surprise, shortly after the New Year's Day, 1977, Ricky and Maria committed to become husband and wife. They had waited for their eighteenth birthdays to marry. We were not sure if it was a good idea, but it was their idea.

Maria and Ricky married quietly, and with little fanfare. They decided to tell their relatives but only after the Justice of the Peace performed the ceremony. Both Maria and Ricky dropped out of school during the regular school day. Maria left school before graduating because of school policy, and Ricky so he could go to work to support his family. They resolved to complete their high school education at night.

Ricky had always wanted to go into law enforcement. He needed a diploma to become a policeman. I asked Ricky, "How are you going to complete high school and get your diploma?"

Ricky responded with maturity, "Maria and I have already talked about that. We both want to finish school. Maria will start night classes first, and I will take care of the baby. Then I will take classes at night while Maria stays home. I promise, Mr. M., we will finish. We will make sure of that."

On a cold, sun-bathed January day in Massachusetts, Maria and Ricky needed witnesses in order to make their marriage official. Megan Straffa and Karla Betts beamed as they stood up for the couple. We, as faculty, did not know what would happen to Maria and Ricky Brezos. They married because a baby was coming. As Megan and Karla wrote in a card celebrating the newlyweds, "Hope lurks in new beginnings. Love from your teachers, Ms. K. and Ms. M."

When Ana and I heard the news about the Brezos' consecrated union, we held hands, looked at each other, and smiled. We understood.

Chapter 28:
Evan

*I*n the middle 1980's, I and some of my colleagues taught Evan Gorges in class. Evan lifted weights, had developed a muscular body. He never smiled. I wondered why.

Evan was not particularly big, about five feet four inches tall, but young people his age would think at least twice before getting into a scrap with him. His behavior was reminiscent of Jason Burro who had enrolled in college and did well academically and athletically. Karla and I surmised that there was no reason why Evan could not follow Jason's path to being a college student. Karla asked me rhetorically, "Mark, Jason emerged from a violent background so why can't Evan make it too?" As usual, Karla was looking out for the welfare of every student.

There were differences, though, between Evan and Jason. Evan's family had a history of some unusually tragic incidents. His parents had suffered the loss of a son and a daughter prior to Evan's tenth birthday. He would occasionally burst out violently both in school and out without an apparent reason or provocation. Evan's violent outbursts in and out of school were troubling for him, his family, and those he attacked. Karla and I understood Jason's behavior, but we did not understand Evan's, even when we thought we did.

Albert Standwicke, one of our school counselors, reported a conversation he had with Evan prior to a tragic incident in which Evan became involved. Bailey High's administration had suspended Evan from school for a variety of infractions. When Evan returned to school, his teachers referred him to Mr. Standwicke for help. Evan reluctantly made an appointment with the counselor.

In his initial meeting with Evan, Mr. Standwicke told me that he asked Evan "Is there anything I can help you with?"

Evan responded, "Nope." Accompanied only by his usual nonchalant repressed facial expression.

"Evan, we need to talk about some things because of your continuing frequent outbursts in school and out. I would like to help you. It is going to cause you some more trouble if things continue the way they have been."

"What do you mean?"

"You punched Gary Meredian in the face two weeks ago and were suspended from school for bloodying his face and breaking his nose. You were also suspended for breaking some other school rules too."

"That ass-hole, Gary, what's his name? Oh, I see, it is Gary Fuck-face. That mother fucker asked for it. So, I gave it to him."

"I wish, Evan, that you would use better language."

"Oh fuck you Mr. Standwicke. Do you want me to tell you what I think or not?"

"I want you to talk to me. Okay, Evan, say it your way. Go ahead Evan."

"Well, like I said, that cock-sucker asked for it and I gave it to him. I punched him in the fuckin face and then I kicked him in the balls. If he pisses me off again, I will mess his face up permanently, and kick him in his nuts so hard that they won't function no more. If that don't work, I will cut his balls off and shove them in his fucking mouth. How's that for telling you how I feel—Mr. Standwicke?"

"Evan, you are hurting—I know that."

"How do you know? Because you are an asshole too. This whole school is a bunch of assholes."

"Well, I know you have lost family members. One of your brothers died in an accident and your seven-year-old sister more recently."

"So?"

"Maybe you are acting out because of that?"

"So, wouldn't you if it happened to your family?"

"Evan, this is not about me."

"What do you want me to do, tell you how I feel?"

"Yes, I would like to know about what you feel and what you think about things."

"Well, I hate people and I hate you for asking me these stupid, fucking questions."

"Why the hatred Evan?"

"God Damn it! I hate my life. My mother has freaked out. She either screams at me and my brother, or just sits there looking out the window at something. I don't know what the fuck she is looking at."

"How about your dad?"

"Since we lost my brother and sister he has been drinking more and more. When he gets real bad drunk he gets mean and gets violent with us. He hit me the other day. I almost hit him back. I should have."

"What else happens Evan?"

"My father just leaves the house when he gets mad. I don't know where he goes. So I don't know what is up anymore. My mother, oh, she just looks off in the distance, so I don't know where she is at in her head and all. I don't know where my father's head is either and where he is at. I am confused. My father leaves the house for a day or two and I don't know where he goes. I don't know which fucking end is up. After my mother just looks out yonder for a while, she cries. Maybe you can help me Mr. Standwicke. Please."

Mr. Standwicke told me at that point Evan broke down and started crying. The tough guy's tears dripped through his frightened teenage body.

Mr. Standwicke continued. "After a minute or two of sobbing, Evan restarted the conversation, 'What should I do Mr. Standwicke? I want to hurt others so they will feel what I feel all the time. What should I do?' Mark, I didn't know what to tell Evan, so I went with what I could come up with. I told him, 'I think the best thing we can do is keep talking. So, if you ever want to talk please call me or just come to see me.' Darn it, Mark, that is all I could think of saying at the time."

Evan took Mr. Standwicke up on his offer and called one day soon after. He could not reach Mr. Standwicke. Albert planned to return Evan's call as soon as he could, but he was meeting with students who also had pressing problems. There was no one else available to help Evan. Budget cuts and other financial decisions had led to a reduction of the counseling staff.

Unable to reach Mr. Standwicke by telephone, Evan started walking to Bailey High to find Mr. Standwicke. Apparently, the act of opening up with his counselor helped to begin a trusting relationship. When he could not find Mr. Standwicke, Evan left a message asking for a meeting.

Cheryl Wattsen later provided additional clues as to how deeply personal events were bothering Evan. In her English class, Cheryl said, "Evan had written a paragraph that earned an A. He described what it was like to see his parents after they heard that another child had died."

Evan wrote in Cheryl's class: "I came home the other day and found my mom and dad crying. Their faces were white like the blood had left their whole bodies. Another child had died.

Another child. I cried tears inside me. I did not want them to see that I cared too. I didn't want them to love me, because I might be gone soon too. Maybe if they didn't love me, they would not cry when I died."

Cheryl continued, "I tried to talk to Evan about what he wrote, but he would not talk with me. After he had developed a relationship with Mr. Standwicke and was willing to talk with him, he would only talk with the person he trusted."

Before Mr. Standwicke was able to return Evan's phone call, or find out where he could be reached, Evan had returned home. Evan found his father's gun in his dresser drawer. He went down stairs and saw his mother sitting there looking off in the distance. He aimed the gun and shot and killed her.

Apparently, without saying a word to anyone, Evan went looking for his father but could not find him. Evan then headed toward the school with the gun and a backpack. By then, a neighbor had notified the police that shots had been heard coming from Evan's home.

A policeman, who had been alerted that a teenager had a gun and was presumed dangerous, saw Evan carrying the gun walking with purpose toward Bailey High. The policeman stopped Evan. Before words could be exchanged, Evan raised his gun. Another policeman who had been called for backup saw what was happening. When Evan raised his gun, the second policeman fired two shots. Evan died in the ambulance on the way to the hospital.

Mr. Standwicke and I met after Evan's death. Albert Standwicke was suffering from what I thought was misplaced guilt. He said, "I could have helped him but I had other students I needed to help. We just have too many students in need with not enough counselors to go around. But I should have helped him but I did not."

"Albert, I think you did all you could do." I tried to provide a rationale for it all, realizing what I said could do nothing to assuage Mr. Standwicke's sense of having failed.

An under-staffed counseling department with too little time to help them all, some of Bailey's emotionally-scarred young people had nowhere to go. The counselors in the school were doing all they could, but the pressures of high school life could be overwhelming. Our school was not the only school or district feeling the pressure of teenagers in trouble. High stakes testing, fear of failure, teen age insecurities—all adding to the stresses. And, then there was Evan who had additional problems reaching deeply into his family.

As we sat on the grass outside the school, neither Mr. Standwicke nor I could at the moment handle the loss of another student. We sat looking into blank space. We both remembered the loss that Megan and Karla felt when Crissy died. Albert and I took Crissy's suicide hard too. Once again, helplessness resulting in hopelessness edged in.

Albert tried in vain to find some kind of explanation for the loss of yet another student. "Some kids are hurting and help is hard to come by. If parents do not have the money, they cannot pay for private therapy. As a result, some kids are leaving us before they have a chance to grow up. We need to help them over the bridge, so they can maneuver through problems and even prosper through the rest of their lives. Sometimes these kids just need a lift. I wasn't available or even able to give Evan the lift he must have needed."

"Albert, you did what you could. And, yes, Albert, sometimes students just need help getting over a hump. You did all you could given the number of students you have to work with."

"I know you are trying to make me feel better, Mark, but at this point I am riddled with guilt. God damn it!"

"I think I know how you feel."

"Maybe you do and maybe you don't. Mark, where do you

226

think Evan was going to go in the school, and what do you think he was going to do when he got there?"

"I don't know, but shortly before I came out to sit with you I received a call from the police station. I was waiting to tell you, but I might as well tell you now."

"What did they say?"

"Evan's gun was not loaded. The police found bullets in his pocket. After he could not find his father, he must have unloaded the gun as he headed for school. And, he did not have any more weapons or ammunition in his backpack."

"Damn it, Mark. He committed suicide. He knew exactly what he was doing. He headed toward school with an unloaded gun. He must have known he would run into a policeman."

"Too many kids are killing themselves Albert, without ever giving life a chance. We need to help them grow up, so they can see that there is hope—that life is worth living. Evan obviously didn't see it that way."

We sat stunned unable to speak. Albert broke the silence, "Geesus Mark, I need help now."

"Albert." I said. "I absolutely do not know what to say."

"I hope we can think of something because I need to talk this out."

"The only thing I can think of is that Ana and I and some teachers from the school get together on Friday nights for dinner and discussion. Whenever we can arrange it, we talk about personal things, public events, teaching and our students. Would you like to join us some time at one of our potluck dinners?"

"Yes, I would. And, Mark, the sooner, the better."

"You know, Albert, most of the kids we work with turn out just fine. It's the ones we lose that penetrate our soul."

"Yah, Mark, it really hurts. Damn it. We win some don't we? Tell me we do."

"Yes, we do. Jason Burro, who had problems with violence and abuse in his background, has graduated from college. As far as we know, he is doing just fine. There are other examples of our students making it. Albert, our work is not futile although it feels like it is at times like this."

"But, we lost Evan. I was not there for him. And, Mark, you know, I did not really know how to be there for him. When the school system first needed a counselor, I raised my hand. I was a math teacher at the time and had a Master's degree. My degree was in math, not in the work I was going to do. I was made a counselor without any expertise whatsoever. I had been teaching for years and was ready to do something else. With a superintendent who valued keeping taxes down to please the school board and the town's legislators, I was hired rather than searching for someone with the requisite education and qualifications which would have necessitated a higher salary.

"I attended a few workshops, took a couple of courses, but I have never been formally educated in the work I am asked to do. Nobody ever questioned if I had the required background. They just assumed I did because I had been doing the job for a while, and I had an office with a sign with my name on the door. So, I really didn't know what to do with Evan. I failed him and the system failed him. The system should have required that I be educated in the field, but it did not. I just went along with it. It was easier that way. As long as nothing like Evan's tragedy ever happens, then we operate as if everything is fine. Mark, right now, I really can't live with myself."

"I wasn't there for Evan either. Albert, you did the best you could under the circumstances."

"Tell me, Mark. Please tell me that Evan did not die in vain."

"Albert. I do not know yet, but...but there must be a lesson in his death somewhere. I am just not sure what it could be. But there must be. I just don't know what it is right now."

"What could we have done, Mark?"

"I don't know. But maybe the dinner I mentioned could help us both. If you can make it, as soon as Ana and I can arrange it, let's talk with our colleagues at a potluck get together. I think that you and I need someone to talk with. Maybe they will have some ideas on what we can and should do now."

"Yah. Let's do it. I will make sure I am there. That would be good. I need it. I need it bad. I really do. I need to talk this thing out. Please Mark, I hope you and Ana can arrange it. Please."

Chapter 29:
Claudia

*A*fter Ken Lewiston went on sick leave in February of 1985, a long-term substitute, Claudia Pace, finished the year. The faculty liked her and respected what she did taking over from and for Ken. The students loved Ken and missed him. His size nine shoes were difficult to fill, but Claudia was able to finish the year Ken started. Even though she could not replace Ken, because nobody could, Claudia proved a reliable and effective substitute for him. In the fall of 1985, we hired Claudia for a full time position in the social studies department.

Claudia stormed through life—strong, powerful, living life with resolve and zeal. She worked out with weights, and ran marathons. Her muscular structure matched her personality. In the school's corridors, students commented covetously about Claudia's full, athletic physique. Her vigorous personality bumped through her classroom each day refreshing her students' youthful curiosity. Yet, Claudia possessed a cloaked vulnerability. Not completely hidden but not seen often either.

Claudia had moved around from location to location. She started teaching in Appalachia in 1974. She was no nonsense, extracting fools with ease. Claudia advocated social justice in a society not always just. She could not stand seeing people pushed around. She could take a lot, but you had better not push her too far. Anyone who abused her students in any way would be on the receiving end of her wrath. Her anger was something you did not want to experience once, much less twice. She wasn't likely to give up. She was one of those people with whom you want to avoid a fight.

I wondered what happened to her in Appalachia, because it was the one subject she seemed reluctant to talk about. After she developed a trusting relationship with the faculty, she slowly and cautiously began to tell us about her background. When she started to talk about her teaching experience in Appalachia, a fragile Claudia broke through.

At one of our Friday potlucks, after Claudia had been with us for over a year, the subject came up. Cheryl asked Claudia, "What happened in Appalachia?"

Claudia had just turned 33 years old when she joined Bailey High's faculty. Except for a few of our colleagues, most of the rest of us were in our early twenties when we started teaching at Bailey. By 1985, our faculty had aged into our thirties and forties. We had grown together and appreciated Claudia's maturity.

After being with us for a while, Claudia appeared more comfortable. The fact she had worked elsewhere, and her previous experience, helped her to read new situations. She was especially good at recognizing non- verbal signals. Within our faculty, Claudia saw safety signs.

"I feel safer with you now." Claudia began as she opened up in response to Cheryl's inquiry, "I am more comfortable with you all and feel like I can talk to you about what happened when I taught in a coal company town in a mountain community in the Appalachian region. I met and worked with some really good people—and I mean good people. They have a keen sense of justice and well-developed common sense. People in the mountain's hollows have earned the wrinkles that have spread through their faces, necks and hands. They are hard-working, friendly, and welcoming. Most of these God-fearing people join in prayer as they fill church aisles and pews on Sundays. Their homes are always open to vulnerable people who need a meal or a hand until they gain control of their lives. The people in the mountain communities intensely love their families, find dignity in work, possess a steely resolve, and are good citizens. The 'hillbilly image' that you get from television and movies is not at all accurate. What the residents of Appalachia lack, though, is the power of ownership. A large percentage of the owners of the land and resources live outside the region without a sustained commitment to the communities from which they draw their profits. Most of the residents work for large companies with home offices based elsewhere.

"Like their parents, I found the kids to be great too. They are street smart and when given an opportunity they excel academically. They really want to learn. However, the company towns were exactly that—company towns—owned and operated by and for the company. The absentee owners sold the coal, and bought their mammoth beach houses off the backs of coal miners. Absentee owners generally take more out of the communities than they put back in as they exploit workers and their families. In most cases, the companies took their money away from the communities they gained it from, leaving little except polluted streams and coal dust for the miners and their families. The owners managed the miners' lives both when they were above ground and underground. As long as they were able to sell the coal and make a lot of money, the owners did not seem to care. What they did care about and fear were outsiders who had other ideas for the people in their community. I was one of those outsiders teaching in a local high school."

Jake injected, "Sounds to me like a lot of towns I have been in or read about. In fact, since I have been in Gorham I have seen how those with wealth run the town for their benefit. They buy and sell the real estate. What really gets to me, though, is that the wealthier members of these communities send their own kids to private schools, become public school board members in towns like Gorham, and then try to make sure we don't educate any revolutionaries much less kids who would want to reform or change things. In that sense, we have a lot of company towns."

"Jake, I don't agree with you on much." Zack said. "But, as a Libertarian, I see it the same way you do that places like Gorham are—in effect—company towns. In almost every town a small group of people own most of the town's real estate, its businesses, and its industries. The owners of the towns use the government to enforce its hegemony. They control the town councils, the school boards, and the planning boards. And, they use the power of government to make sure it stays that way."

"I see what you mean Jake and Zack. But the company towns I am talking about were even more tightly controlled than Gorham. Gorham, and other towns like it, may be run by a few but it is not as absolute as the company towns I am talking about, at least not yet. Although from what I have seen, Gorham has a lot of the same attributes as company towns."

"Claudia, why don't the people in the town you worked in just leave?" Zack asked. "They are free to leave aren't they?"

"Not really, Zack. They don't have money to go elsewhere. Besides, land, place, and family are important to them so they want to stay in their communities. Some of the locals, who have enough money to tide them over for a while if they leave, do go to find a job elsewhere. However, they usually return home for the simple reason that it is home. They want to smell that mountain air again. And, besides, as I said, and as those who did return told me— 'it is home.'"

"I see what you mean, Claudia. But, I believe in freedom and what you are telling us rips at my soul."

"I get it Zack. However, some of the residents couldn't leave even if they wanted to because they were deeply in debt to the company store where many bought their groceries on credit. If it looked like the debtors were getting ready to leave town, the sheriff and his many deputies showed up. It wasn't pretty when the authorities put the fear of Hades into defenseless families. Rebels were identified and blackballed when they tried to get a job elsewhere and then had no place to go. Most people in the company towns learned to do what they were told and keep quiet in order to keep their jobs and feed their families. These folks went along because taking care of their families was the priority. Like I said—they were good people trying to do what they thought was necessary for their loved ones."

"I thought there were no more company towns in coal country. What you describe sounds like they are still around. So are there still company towns?" Jake asked

"Jake, they might not call them company towns anymore and not too many were still functioning as full-fledged company towns, but the town I was in had the attributes of a company town. The company still controlled things. So, even though more recently you could pay in cash rather than script, there weren't any grocery or department stores close to the mining towns. The companies controlled the towns' various planning boards, so department and grocery stores were zoned way out of town. You didn't have any real choice of where to shop, especially without a car. Cash might just as well be script because you still had to shop in the company stores. You basically did not have a choice."

John pushed for further clarification, "How did all this affect you as a teacher and the schools? Were you able to help in any way?"

Before Claudia could respond, Charles jumped in. "I appreciate, Claudia, you have a story to tell. The problem is, as usual, there is another side. I have been to Appalachia. The coal industry provides a lot of jobs. The people there like jobs. They like their life there or else they would leave. I think that answers your earlier question, Zack. I understand your inquiry, yours Jake, yours too John, and the rest of you. But, as I like to keep reminding all of you, there is another side."

"Charles, there is another side. Coal does provide jobs, but I believe at a significant human price. Some of the older miners suffer from 'black lung' disease and other afflictions as a result of breathing coal dust and other chemicals."

"Okay, but after you finish, Claudia, I will probably have more to say."

"I am sure you will, Charles." Megan said.

"To answer John's question, the company's ideology controlled the schools too. I grew up in a family where independence of thought was valued. I went to a private, independent college where critical thinking was encouraged. When I went into teaching, I decided to teach in Appalachia because I wanted to make a difference. In my progressive high school and in college, I read Michael Harrington's *The Other America*, learned about the presidencies of Kennedy and Johnson, and the 'Great Society.' So, I thought I might be able to help the kids and families in Appalachia. I was idealistic, I know, but I thought I could help."

John followed up, "What happened? Were you able to change anything?"

"First, let me tell you what I and other teachers were up against. There is some history to the story. In the early 1970's, in part because of the gains made in the civil rights movement, there was more freedom in the society at large. In some parts of Appalachia, however, mining communities were interested in keeping the 'free thinking' of some in the outside world out of their schools. Kids who could think for themselves may rebel against the company town's way of doing things. Furthermore, people in the energy producing towns still knew where their paychecks came from. During the first half of the twentieth century, when coal was king, mine owners ruled the company towns. The company owned the houses its workers and their families lived in. The company owned the stores, the workers' families purchased in them, prices were high, and the company's products had to be paid for by company issued script that could only be used in company-owned stores."

"Didn't the state governments in Appalachia try to help the people?" Jake asked.

"Well, first, the state capitals are sometimes miles away from the mining communities and some legislators are convinced that what they hear is hearsay. Second, the natural resource industries—coal, oil, timber, and natural gas contribute heavily to those who want to get elected and re-elected to the various states' legislatures. The elected government officials had to raise campaign money in order to get elected and then re-elected. Money is the life-blood of the American political system. You cannot get elected without it. So, candidates garner campaign money from those who have it. And, you stay in office if those who have money are pleased with what you do. This is Political Science 101, following the money."

"How about the appointed officials? Were they any better?" John asked.

"Generally, the same people who were elected through industry contributions were the ones who nominated and confirmed the bureaucrats."

"Couldn't the federal government step in?" Megan asked.

"Some federal agencies tried. For example, the Environmental Protection Agency, which had been established in 1970, tried to get the pollution reduced. But state governments often fought the EPA and its efforts at regulating the polluting industries. The politicians would scream 'Jobs, jobs, jobs. We need jobs. The federal government is trying to take away our ways to put bread on the table for our families.' So politically, federal regulation was very hard to implement. There were other problems with pollution."

"What were those Claudia?" Jake asked.

"Well, some industries up river dumped their waste into the rivers that flowed downstream into the southern-most counties of Appalachia. We had some kids in class from the hollows with learning difficulties. We, as teachers, speculated that there might be something in the water. Water tainted with certain pollutants is not good for young people, or anyone for that matter, to drink or even to bathe in."

"Was the water tainted?" Jake followed.

"I am not sure. It seemed that investigations were delayed when investigators got close to proving that economically important companies were involved in polluting rivers and streams. Because of the pollution, water flowed into the hollows, people living there drank and cooked with the water, and opportunities for sanitation were finite. Folks with some money bought homes on the higher ground, where the slurry ran downhill away from their homes with a view. Those with real money, the owners of the companies, lived elsewhere only visiting Appalachia to extract their profits. As I mentioned earlier, the EPA was not welcomed in the community I lived and worked in. I believe that was also the case in other communities around where I taught."

"Were the companies successful in preventing environmental regulation from being enforced, Claudia?"

"Yes, some were, Jake, for the most part they were. There wasn't much enforcement. Claims were made that some regulators looked the other way—so to speak."

"Oh, damn, this is worse than I thought." Megan said.

"Claudia, what will happen to the people who work the mines if coal does not provide them with jobs?" Cheryl asked.

"I don't know. As I said, these are good people working in the mining industry who are trying to make an honest living. They provide food for their families through mining coal and working in associated businesses. They send their children to school and college through their earnings. I don't know what they would do for jobs if the coal mining industry was no longer their main source of income. In some of the communities, there aren't many jobs that are not associated in some way with the coal industry. The people who live and work there have no place they want to go even if they could. Home is home to them. As I said, the owners of the mines generally have second homes elsewhere. Consequently, most of the owners can cut and run when things get tough. They can take the profits they have excavated from the mountains and buy another industry somewhere else. The workers don't have that option. So, Cheryl, I don't know what they will do but I believe the folks who live there deserve a whole lot more than they are receiving."

"Please tell us more, Claudia. This is a learning experience, not necessarily a pleasant one—but I am learning." I said.

"Well, back to the company towns. Historically, the companies' guards, who were often called sheriffs—official or not, were paid for by the public but controlled by the companies. The politicians made sure it stayed that way. The sheriffs made sure there was no stealing. And, if there was theft, a beating on the way to solitary confinement was the least of it. Jail times were usually for indefinite periods. If you ever did get to see a judge, many of the judges saw it the way the company owners did. There were often no sentences—recalcitrant miners were just jailed for an indeterminate amount of time—some even died in the dank, damp, freezing-cold jail cells. Those who lived through their imprisonment were usually fined, came out of jail with debt, and had to pay the debt fast. Interest rates were high, compounded frequently, necessitating the debtor to become further indebted to the company. After jail time, company doctors often treated those who had been incarcerated for infections and rat bites. Medicines were scarce. Some prisoners lost limbs as a result of disease and gangrene. There was no social security safety net or anything resembling one prior to 1935.

"So, in effect, in the early part of the 1900's, the company towns had company judges and their own company controlled guards. There were no juries or courts for appeals. Of course, there were no appeals." Claudia ended with a pained laugh.

I asked, "Claudia, how could you stand it even for a couple of years? Haven't things changed?"

She continued, almost ignoring that I had spoken. Claudia was rolling through the telling of her story. "Furthermore, the company's employees read incoming mail to make sure there were no 'subversives' within the camps or out waiting to come in. Company censors made sure that any available newspapers printed stories that favored the company's view of life. When anyone tried to form a union, company owners blocked and obstructed such attempts. If obstruction didn't work, then efforts were made to undermine the union. Company spies identified anyone who even looked pro-union or spoke for unionizing. The companies dealt with those perceived as union organizers. Much of the sabotaging was successful. If preventing worker actions didn't work, then maybe a beating or two would be incentive enough to just shut up and do what the company tells you to do. If that wasn't successful in breaking a man and his family, then the miner was given further physical encouragement to leave town. If that didn't work—who knows what could happen to a recalcitrant inhabitant of a company town. The companies either owned the news outlets or influenced them in other ways through advertising revenue or editorial board members, so what was reported the company almost always sanctioned. Periodically, news that could actually help miners and their families seeped through. Although, monitors watched carefully to make sure workers did not receive much less read any rebellious literature. Anything advocating unions received special attention. This occurred right up to when World War II broke out—maybe even after.

"Mark, you asked if things have changed. Yes, they have somewhat. There are no longer as many company towns as there once were. Today, they aren't usually called company towns anymore. But, they are de facto company towns. Run by, for, and of the elites who govern them. As I mentioned, the elites control the towns from a distance—primarily, now through political contributions. As far as I could tell, the way things were done when I was there were not much different from what the historians tell us the towns were like in the first half of the twentieth century."

"So much for change," I said with about as much sarcasm as I could muster.

Claudia continued, "Even some of the town's preachers made sure that their parishioners understood that their reward was awaiting them, but not on this earth. In this 'real' world, it was the company owner's heaven."

Chapter 30:
"Company Schools"

"Claudia, how about the schools, did the company control those too?" I asked.

"Yes. Mark. We, the teachers, were kept on a short leash. There were anti-worker and anti-union snoops among us who would do what they could to divide and conquer any who dared to rebel, think out loud about doing so, or even look like they might be unmanageable. Anyone who questioned the status quo and was perceived as having the power to do something to change anything, including teachers, was told, 'Get out of town and don't come back.' I got that message. I loved the kids, I loved the people, but the controllers of the town did not love me.

"In addition, I made the mistake of living in a corporate owned house. It was cheaper, but I lost some of my freedom. I was expected to be a 'good girl'—translated— 'don't make any trouble.' Once they realized I might be a problem, everything I did at home and in the town was watched, observed, and noted." At this point, strong, stoic, tough Claudia's defenses disintegrated. Her eyes flooded.

After a pause, which seemed like an eternity, Claudia composed herself and continued, "At the time I started teaching, in the early 1970's, textbook controversies were affecting what was happening in classrooms in some

Appalachian states and elsewhere in the country. Some parents believed the public schools were doing the work of the devil. Kids talked about what they were learning in class, alarming some influential residents. The parents and citizens with power scolded the school boards. As a result, school officials called for the schools that were teaching anything except the approved curriculum, meaning the non-controversial that favored the established powers, to be censured and the books censored."

"Refresh our memory. What was so controversial?" I asked.

"Any book, any film, any instructional material that did not fit into the approved, in my judgement, restrictive curriculum mandated by a 'conserve the way it has always been' school board, could not be used in the classroom. It is important for you to know that I worked with some great teachers. They realized that they were preparing students for the outside world, and because of the limited opportunities in the coal mining industry, these teachers offered their students a view outside a mine shaft. The English teachers helped the students learn that the accent they spoke with in their communities was fine and perfectly acceptable. However, the outside world had a different accent and they should know both."

John asked, "Claudia, you taught history there, right?"

"Yes, I did, but the assistant principal responsible for the curriculum sanitized the history we were supposed to teach."

"Spell that out for me."

"Well, we weren't supposed to talk too much about the 'Mine Wars' from 1912 to 1921. We weren't supposed to talk about unions, at least not favorably. We weren't supposed to talk about a lot of things that actually happened."

"Did you try to teach about what really occurred in history?" Jake asked.

"Yes, I did. At first, I tried to sneak more historical truth into my classes. Then I started being more explicit. That is what eventually got me into trouble: trying to provide students with the whole truth and nothing but."

"Please go on Claudia. In most school systems I know of in the United States, the history curriculum is designed to communicate the rosy version of a given community's history." Zack said.

Jake added, "Like here in Gorham. For the most part, we can teach United States history without significant intervention. Of course, we need to follow the curriculum, but we do have some freedom. When it comes to local history, though, we have to teach 'celebratory' history because that version helps to sell homes and products in Gorham, Massachusetts."

"Zack and Jake, I agree with what you are both saying. Furthermore, the company schools where I taught in Appalachia prepared students for life in the company's towns. No dissent was allowed. The place I experienced was not what you read about in some of the novels or see in some of the movies where young people rebel and escape from their pre-determined fate. Of course, some do, but most don't. Without an education, the kids I taught were mostly heading for the mines or jobs in support of the mines. A teacher, or anyone else, best not get in the way of the train going under-ground—especially, anyone who came from the outside of the mining way of doing things. If you did try to change things, then you were perceived as a subversive to the mining way of life. The pipeline from the schools to the mines, or under-educated to the mines, determined what these kids' lives would be like. The kids could have become educated if we gave them a chance. The students I had in class were really smart. I tried to change things. I wanted to introduce new ideas, new books, and different ways to live. In company towns, everything was controlled, and you were well-advised to not go against the company. 'Spies' operated everywhere. Often, without meaning to, kids would go home to their parents and tell them what the teacher said, or they thought the teacher said, or what they were learning in class. If what I and others were teaching was perceived as critical to the company, then the word got back to the bosses. The boss rewarded those with information, especially information that the company could use to eradicate 'subversives.' Also, the paternalistic company did things for you if you did what the managers wanted you to do. The company handed out bonuses to those who helped keep the lid on. It was clear that those who do things for you also control you. I did not like the control. The company 'managed' the school board. The school board soon grew to dislike me, and even fear what I was doing. I eventually had no choice but to leave."

"That sounds like leaving was a really good idea." Megan interjected.

"Yes, Megan, I thought at first that it was a good idea too. I left, but then the kids didn't have their teacher. I felt and still feel bad about that. Maybe I should have stayed—gutted it out. But the people who owned the communities didn't like outsiders messing around with their property—material and human. Any sign of rebellion was crushed."

"What about the unions? Couldn't they help?"

"When and where there were unions, the unions did what they could. But the companies, with the tacit support, and sometimes the overt support of the state legislatures, weakened the unions. Sometimes the unions were rendered so ineffective that they were united in name only. Without strong union support, there was no place for the workers and their families to go for assistance."

"How about the students? How did they respond to what you

were trying to do?" Cheryl asked.

"Well, that is complicated and important. Most of the students said they liked the classes I taught. As far as I could tell, they were telling me the truth and not just buttering me up. The students told me that they learned in my classes because the content was relevant to their lives and the teaching methods were different from what they usually experienced.

"Yet, some of the students who seemed to be into what we were doing in class were absent a lot. I was never sure why there were so many absences, but it did not help the learning process. And then the administrators intervened when I tried to provide life options. Of course, things like field trips to see a different part of world were out of the question. The administrators used expense as an excuse, but when I offered to raise money for trips they just said 'no.' No reason was given to me, or apparently thought necessary."

"Yikes. Seeing the outside world seems like a good idea—field trips—life options. Wow!" Karla said. "We could use some creativity in this world. Doing something different. Especially changing things where you were teaching. It doesn't seem as if the kids had a chance. Was it coal or nothing?"

"You see, Karla, the coal mine owners had an inexpensive source of labor in male teenagers. They did not want to lose it. If these students saw something different, pursued other life options and went away to school or moved to another community where there was a diversified economy, then the supply of labor would be less. As a result, the owners would have to pay more for workers; thus, cutting into their profit margins. That was not part of their business model. Keeping these kids isolated was part of the overall plan; therefore, the young people had few choices. Staying and working in the mines became the only choice which was really no choice at all.

"In addition, in mining, production often prevailed over

safety. Many miners were injured on the job, and when there was no disability insurance, some of them just withered away. These men in their early fifties, and they were mostly men but there were some women, were considered by management to be getting too old to work fast. They were just let go. Teenagers dropped out of school to take their places. After the unemployment checks ended, the unemployed workers in their early fifties searched for income. Most were not yet eligible for a minimal social security check. Miners who had been injured were often laid off. Those with serious injuries all too often lived the rest of their lives on painkillers. Out of work and on disability, some of the residents used narcotics to ease their pain and to delay worries. In order to make life tolerable, they frequently retreated into alcohol or drugs after brief periods of sobriety. Treatment centers for addiction were scarce and under-resourced. It is not a pretty picture. Is it my friends and colleagues?"

"No Claudia, it isn't. To this point you have been talking mostly about the men. What happened to the women in the towns?" Megan asked.

"Some women worked in mining-related jobs and were in the front lines of resistance whether it was in work stoppages or providing crucial intelligence to those organizing labor groups. Yet, women also had the job of raising the children. Therefore, the women who didn't have an income-producing job 'should just stay at home having babies and taking care of them.' This, in addition to taking care of 'their man.' Of course, getting married limited life options for both the husband and the wife. Further schooling was generally not an option when babies came along."

"Oh, my God. Once again, women abused and subjugated. Damn it. Damn it. Damn it!" Megan couldn't keep it in any longer.

"Come on Megan. You are being a drama queen again. Didn't Claudia also say that women were active in the labor movement? So, it wasn't that bad." Charles said.

"Charles, once again, you have gone over the top. You really irritate me sometimes, actually, most of the time."

"Mark, can I talk without being interrupted?" Charles asked. "Well, first, I appreciate your story Claudia, but there is another side."

"What is that Charles?" Claudia responded.

"As I said earlier, coal provides jobs for people. The miners value the camaraderie they develop with each other. I thought you liberals value people joining together for a common purpose. Also, what the miners do provides inexpensive energy for those of us who live on the east coast. I believe those are good things. I believe you would agree. Wouldn't you?"

"I agree with some of what you said, but not all of it." Claudia answered. "But, go ahead, Charles."

"I will. Furthermore, surface mining, or as some people call it, 'strip mining,' is safer. Aren't all you 'libs' in favor of safer mining as well as miner camaraderie? I don't want you limousine liberals to get weak-kneed on me." Charles said with a satisfied smirk.

"But that kind of mining destroys mountain tops."

"The companies are making the mountain tops serve other purposes by building schools and other public facilities on top of the flat surfaces. So, it isn't all negative as you 'tree huggers' depict it. Anyway, I don't want to be too critical, but if you liked the kids and the people so much, Claudia, why did you leave?"

"I get your point Charles, but even though I loved the kids and the people the final straw for me was what happened to a really good guy who was a great educator. At the time, he was an assistant principal. I will use his first name, Jeff. He really cared about the kids. He was the one administrator I met there who supported the hopes and desires of students rather than the coal mine owners."

"It sounds as if Jeff was doing some good things in the school you were in. What happened that affected you so much, Claudia?" I asked.

"Well, I had gotten to know him professionally. We would have coffee together. The kids were first with him. The students liked him a lot. He was not afraid to help them. He was not one of those administrators who came down on me. In fact, he seemed to be protecting me so the kids in my classes could learn."

"Sounds good to me." Megan said.

"I shouldn't have told you even his first name. Please don't mention his name outside of this group, or anything about him."

"Claudia, we are firm about keeping our discussions within this group. We don't talk about what we say in our potlucks." I said. "So, please don't worry. You can feel free to talk candidly in this group."

"Okay, Mark. For those kids who planned to stay in the hollows and in the mining communities, Jeff tried to help them improve their lives even if they stayed where they were. For some of the students who wanted to leave, he worked with them on how to get out of the town after they graduated from high school. He helped some of them get into college and obtain financial assistance."

"So, how did he get into trouble?" Cheryl asked.

"Well, some powerful people in the community heard that Jeff was a buffer between the company's ideology and the kids. As I said, the company had a ready source of cheap labor as long as these teenagers did not leave town. Jeff saw that I was trying to help my students see an alternate future, so he stood between me and some other administrators and staff who were watching out for the company's interests. Without us ever talking about it, because it would be dangerous to do so, Jeff was a fellow quiescent rebel. He tried to keep the wolves at bay. He protected me while he could, but Jeff was not careful enough about his own survival. The guys, and yes they were mostly guys, who ran the towns had the formal and informal power. They had money and they used it to get things done, politically and legally if they could—and in whatever ways that were necessary if they believed they had to."

"Isn't this the good ole U. S. of A. where you have rights?" Megan asked.

"Megan, it is hard to fathom how connected these owners are. With coal being a resource, they are politically and economically inter-connected in-state, inter-state, nationally, and yes, internationally."

"What happened with Jeff then?" I asked.

"A student came into his office one day and closed the door. Jeff talked to a lot of students behind slightly ajar doors. In this case, the student closed the door entirely and Jeff left it closed. Even an ajar door was probably a bad practice for a good looking guy like Jeff, but it was a common practice at the school among administrators when privacy was necessary."

"So, what was the problem?" I wasn't getting the point and wanted Claudia to explain further.

"Well, Mark, the student, a sixteen-year-old female who had met with Jeff in his office with the door closed went to the principal the next day and claimed that Jeff touched her."

"Did he and what happened after?" I followed.

"He was summarily fired."

"Without a hearing?" I asked.

"Yah, Mark, in company towns without a strong union you don't get a hearing. Furthermore, Clara, the student, came to me a week later badly shaking and in tears. Without my asking her, she told me that Jeff never touched her."

"WHAT?" Megan blurted out.

"Yes, Megan, all of this is hard to believe. Clara told me that two men told her that her unemployed and perennially out-of-work father would get a job if she would go in to see Jeff and then claim he touched her."

"So, he was framed so to speak. Right?" I asked.

"Right. Clara said that her father needed work. The family had no money and 'Food Stamps,' as they were called at the time, were not enough to feed a family of eight—so her dad needed the job. She agreed to say Jeff touched her, but did not think that Jeff would be accused of touching her in a 'sexual way.' As tears filled her cheeks, Clara told me that 'He never even touched me'. By the time she was ready to recant her story, Jeff had been fired. They got him. He had pissed some powerful people off, because I believe, he was trying to help these kids improve their lives. For the most part, parents supported what Jeff was trying to do. Entrenched interests in the town did not. So they got him."

Megan had heard enough, "Bastards. Those bastards."

"Ditto!" Said Karla.

"Oh, come on, Megan and you too Karla, and everyone else. Let's control the drama." Charles said. "It is just the way it is. So let's not get too excited. We need the coal and the energy. We also need the miners to extract it, and companies to hire them and finance its exploration. So, let's just relax. Okay."

As Megan seethed at Charles' comments, I asked Claudia, "What ever happened to Jeff? And, did Clara tell the truth eventually?"

"I never have heard from Jeff or anything about what happened in his life. I hope he didn't leave education. He was a good one. As far as Clara is concerned, she dropped out of school shortly after the incident. We have not talked since that time. I did not try to reach out to her nor did she try to contact me."

"Were you afraid with what you knew?" I asked.

"Yes. After I left the area, I got married. After three years of marriage, I got divorced. I kept my married name. In part, so I could not be tracked. Those company guys run things down there. They have power—power to ruin the reputations of people who want to change what they have and the way they have it. They could come after me so I have remained quiet."

"Are you ever going to tell what Clara told you?"

"Besides telling you all, I don't know. I am still afraid. Even though it was a while ago that this happened, and I have moved, and I have a new name, I am still afraid. I probably shouldn't even be telling you about this."

"Claudia, they really did scare the shit out of you." Megan said.

"Yah. They did. I haven't told you the kicker. About two years after I left the area, and even though I had changed my name, I received an anonymous letter that warned me that 'If you ever show up in these parts again, you would be arrested. We would LOVE to get you in jail!' I don't know how they found me but they did."

"What. What the hell could you possibly be arrested for?" Karla asked.

"Oh, I don't know. Maybe a dirty windshield wiper, or an improperly tinted window, or a brake light that wasn't really out was 'out', if you know what I mean. Or maybe a crooked license plate, or a slanted headlight, or if I said anything that could be perceived as being disrespectful, then I could be facing a 'resisting arrest' charge. The list goes on."

"And, Claudia, I can just imagine what the letter meant by 'LOVE to get you in jail.'" Megan said.

"If the alleged 'crooked license plate,' that was claimed to be unreadable, was not enough to keep me in jail then I, like Jeff, could be accused of inappropriately touching a student. You see, maybe because I worked out and had muscles, and I had heard the term 'Butch' muttered as some people walked by, I thought that maybe someone would use a trumped up charge of sexual abuse against me. I was getting paranoid."

"This is all so bizarre. How could they do that?" Cheryl said.

"The rumor was that I was indiscriminate. The rumor-mongers claimed that I liked both boys and girls. I guess you can all see why I am afraid and haven't been back."

"Claudia, I certainly get it." Cheryl said. "But what happens to the kids who are still in those communities?"

"I don't know, but I am afraid that some of them really don't have a chance from the get go. Maybe I should have stayed there and gutted it out."

"Megan, you wanted to say something else." I said.

"Yah. I don't see the schools in Gorham, Massachusetts as being much different. Look what happened to Derek Randallston. He did not have a fair hearing and he was drummed out of town. The way I see it—there are a lot of company schools throughout the United States of America."

"If Megan is correct about company schools—that there are lots of them in communities throughout our country—then that means that school curricula are implicitly directed to a company's preconceived ends. So much for independent and critical thought if what school systems are doing is serving the interests of a given industry. It might be the natural resource industries in Appalachia, large manufacturing plants that provide jobs in the Midwest, the technology corridors in the northeast, or the migrant farms on the west coast. Formidable industries influence, if not outright control, what happens in schools. I get the point that Megan makes and that Claudia has been making." Zack said.

"Furthermore, we have the phenomenon we have discussed before—in addition to what Claudia has been talking about the school to the mines pipeline we have the school to the prison pipeline. We have kids suspended from school, they then get into trouble in the streets, and go to prison and never get out of the criminalized syndrome." Megan added.

Our potluck for the evening was about to end. Ana and I still had to schedule a potluck when Albert Standwicke could join us. In the future, we have so much more to do. Yet, as in previous Friday night dinners, we had delved into crucial issues. Most Bailey High students reach their goals, often exceeding them. Some have to overcome difficulties and succeed in doing so. Jason Burro has quelled his past and is advancing in life. Maria and Ricky Brezos are married and working on their educations. Other students have not fared as well. Yes, there are problems but if we do not face them and work through them then who would be there for our students. I get frustrated but frustration can lead to change.

Once more, I did not know what to say or do, so I appealed to my colleagues for any suggestions or proposals, "Clearly, we have some problems that Claudia has helped us to highlight. The challenges are everywhere. Even here in Gorham, maybe especially here in Gorham. Any thoughts?" I asked.

"No Mark, I have no idea what we should or can do now. It just seems hopeless. Anyone else have any ideas? Jake asked.

"Mark, Jake, and the rest of you. You all can't just give up, because who would then be able to help the kids?" Ana said.

"Well, we all need to think about what is happening in our schools. We need to figure out what we can do to help make our teaching and our schools better. The best thing we can do, I believe, is get ready for school on Monday and do the best we can."

"Mark, is that enough?"

"I don't know Megan. I don't know. But, Megan, it is all we have."

Karla, though, knew what she thought, "TEACHER—what a great word. I am so proud to be one. I love the concept of teaching. I am passionate about what we do each and every day. When someone introduces me as a teacher, I savor the sound of the word.

"HEY, everyone, regardless the odds against us, we have to do what we can—our best. I know most of the kids have parents behind them. But when they come into school with parents behind them or not, we are it for them. A teacher educates regardless the obstacles. I love my students—each and every one of them. Even though we have all these problems confronting us, I can't wait to get back to school on Monday. We may not be able to do everything, but we can certainly do something. We teach. That is what we do. Every day is a new beginning. Every student offers us an opportunity to help a young person learn. Bring it on."

"I am in it for the long haul," I said.

"Me too—Mr. M.—Me too."

Mr. M's Notebook: A Teacher's Life continues in Book Two. Book 2 is subtitled, "High School." The tentative publication date for book 2 is in 2018.

CPSIA information can be obtained
at www.ICGtesting.com
Printed in the USA
FFOW02n1920121116
29240FF